What's Behind
The
Screen Door?

By

SUSAN L. PARE'

What's Behind the Screen Door?   by Susan L. Paré

MORE BOOKS BY THIS AUTHOR

Red

The House on Ludington Street

The Mayor's Son

Willerton Woods

Cowtown

Floating Face Down
A Sheriff "Cowboy" Berkson Mystery Novel – Book Three

Let's Play Autopsy

A Bad Week In Hollister
A Sheriff "Cowboy" Berkson Mystery Novel – Book Two

Don't Smother Your Mother
A Sheriff "Cowboy" Berkson Mystery Novel – Book One

Crossing Sydney

Blueberries and Bears and My Brother's Shoes
First Edition – out of print

What's Behind the Screen Door?   by Susan L. Paré

Contents

What's Behind The Screen Door?

by

SUSAN L. PARE'

2001

2

One

"For crying out loud, Marg. Will you please put some clothes on?"

Marg turned and glanced back at her husband, Michael, who was sitting at the kitchen table eating his breakfast. She grinned at him.

"I will in a few minutes. I just got out of the shower. I'm air drying."

"Is that what you're doing? It looks to me like you're doing the dishes in the nude."

"I'm multi-tasking, Sweetie. I can do more than one thing at a time, you know."

Marg reached for the hand towel that was lying next to her on the countertop. She turned, as she dried her hands, and stared at Michael.

Michael Finnegan laid his fork on his plate and stared back at her. "How long is this going to go on, Marg? I hardly see you with clothes on anymore."

Marg smiled flirtatiously at him. "Hey, just remember that going to that nudist colony was your idea. I can't help it if I discovered that I enjoyed going without clothes. Anyway, I thought you enjoyed looking at my naked body," she replied.

"I did. I mean, I do. But I'd like to see you in some clothes once in a while."

Marg laughed. "I get dressed every day. You know that."

Michael looked at her questioningly. "You do get dressed right after I leave, don't you?"

"Of course, I do. My god, Michael, what do you

think? That I clean the house and go shopping without any clothes on?"

Michael grinned. "That would be a sight to see. Little Margie Finnegan walking down the isles in the grocery store, naked as a jaybird, picking out cucumbers and bananas."

Marg grinned. "And, just what would I be needing those for when I have you?"

Michael was suddenly aware that he had become hard. He reached over and pulled her onto his lap. "Let's go upstairs. I think I can be a little late this morning. After all, I am the boss."

Marg took his hand and placed it between her legs. "Here," she murmured.

"What?"

"Here. On the table."

Michael only hesitated a second before he shoved his dirty plate aside, picked up his wife, and sat her on the table facing him. He undid his trousers and let them drop to the floor. Marg wrapped her arms around his neck and smiled. "Now, aren't you glad I didn't get dressed?" she asked him, speaking softly.

Michael pushed her back onto the table, spread her legs, and quickly entered her. "I do now," he exclaimed.

Seconds later, Michael groaned and collapsed on top of her. "Sorry," he whispered. "I couldn't hold back."

Marg pushed him off of her and sat up on the edge of the table. "That's all right, Sweetie. There's always tonight."

At eleven o'clock, the doorbell rang. Marg smiled as she opened the door. "I wondered if I was going to get any mail today," she said, teasingly.

"You're dressed," he said, surprised.

"I was just leaving. I've got to go grocery shopping."

"But. . . I mean. . ." he stuttered.

"What?"

"I was looking forward to. . ."

Marg laughed as she grabbed his tie. "Get in here," she said, as she pulled him into the house. "And, don't look so disappointed. The shopping can wait."

Marg answered the door and took the small package from the UPS driver. "Thanks. Do I need to sign for the package?"

He grabbed his crotch and grinned. "You mean this package?" he asked, as he stepped into the living room.

"Aren't you the funny man?" she said, joking. "How much time do you have?" Marg inquired, watching him as he undid his trousers and let them drop to the floor.

"I'm a little ahead of schedule, but I need to be out of here by three at the latest."

Marg let her robe drop to the floor.

"God, you're beautiful," he said, as he reached out and pulled her closer.

She looked down and grinned. "I do enjoy the little packages you bring me."

The UPS driver laughed. "Little? I'd hate to see

what you call big if you think this is little?" he said, as he pulled her down onto the couch.

"Geez, you scared the crap out of me," Marg shouted. "What the hell are you doing here? It's not Wednesday."

He stared at her, his eyes blazing with fury. "You fucking slut!"

"Did anyone see you come in?" she asked, glancing out the window.

"That's what you're concerned about? I just saw the UPS driver leave. Why aren't you concerned that someone saw him come in?" he shouted.

"He was just leaving a package," she uttered softly.

"What the hell do you take me for? An idiot? You were screwing him, Marg. I've been in the kitchen for the past five minutes watching you."

She locked eyes with him and smirked. "So, what if I was? Do you seriously believe that you're the only man in my life?" She turned away from him and started to walk into the dining room. "God, you're so pathetic. You make me sick, you pervert. Just leave, will you?"

He followed her, grabbed her arm, and pulled her towards him. "Oh, I'm leaving, all right. But, before I leave, you're gonna give me one hell of a fantastic blow job."

"The hell I am," Marg shouted. "Now, get your sorry ass out of my house."

He grabbed her flimsy robe and tore it off of her. "Get on your knees," he demanded.

As her hand came forward to slap him, he pushed her away from him. She gave him a surprised look as she fell backward, hitting her head on the edge of the dining room table.

The man looked down at her and realized that she was out cold. "Shit," he muttered to himself. He checked her wrist for a pulse. Nothing. He held his breath as he put his fingers on the carotid artery on the side of her neck. He smiled when he felt a pulse. She was alive.

He started to stand, then, hesitated as the memory of seeing her with the UPS driver flashed through his mind. His anger came rushing back and he swung a leg over her body, straddling her. He put his hands around her neck and stared down at her face. Then, he tightened his grip around her neck and slowly squeezed the life out of her naked body.

Exhausted, he sat back on his haunches and took a few deep breaths. He glanced around the room, crawled off her, and stood up. He reached down, grabbed her robe, and wiped down all the surfaces that he recalled touching while in the house. He threw the robe on a chair in the living room and left.

At four-thirty that afternoon, Lyle Sleeter rang the Finnegans' doorbell. When no one answered, he put his face on the screen door and looked into the living room.

"Mrs. Finnegan," he yelled through the screen door. "It's Lyle Sleeter. I'm here to collect for the newspaper."

There was no answer.

Lyle knew she was home. The front door was open and he knew she never left the house without locking all the doors.

He hesitated for a second, then opened the door and entered the house. He looked around, wondering where she was.

"Marjorie? Are you home?"

The fifteen-year-old boy stood in the middle of the living room, hoping to hear some noise to indicate where she might be in the house.

He wasn't sure if he should look for her or leave. He certainly didn't want to be caught in her house without her being there. He glanced into the dining room and saw her lying on the floor. "Shit!" he exclaimed, as he ran over to her. He stared at her naked body and immediately felt aroused and embarrassed at the same time.

"Marjorie, are you all right?" he asked, his voice almost a whisper.

He couldn't take his eyes off her breasts. He'd seen them before, but this was different. Being aware of his erection and feeling ashamed, he forced himself to look away.

It was then he saw the blood. He started to feel nauseous and fought the desire to vomit. He backed away from her, turned, and started to run out of the room. Suddenly, he hesitated, reached into his back pocket, and pulled out his cell phone. He slowly walked back into the dining room, glanced down at her, and took a picture.

Two

Sheriff Richard Tickman stood up and glanced into the living room. Michael Finnegan had not moved. He was sitting in the same chair he had been in when Tickman arrived. His face was buried in his hands and he was sobbing. Tickman decided to give him a few more minutes before trying, once again, to question him.

"What do you think, Doc? Any idea of what happened?"

The coroner, Dr. William Galante, was kneeling over the body of Marjorie Finnegan. He looked up at the sheriff. "It's obvious that she has a head wound, but I don't think that's what killed her."

"Was she raped?" the sheriff whispered, not wanting Michael Finnegan to hear him.

"I won't know for sure until I get her on the table, but seeing as how she's naked, there's a good chance she was." The coroner groaned as he stood. "I'm getting old, Tic. These old bones are starting to wear out."

"We're all getting old, Doc."

The coroner looked at the sheriff. "God, you're tall. I get a stiff neck every time I look at you."

Sheriff Tickman smiled. "You say that every time you see me."

"I know. But, for some reason, I seem to forget how big you are until I see you again. It's always a little shock. Anyway, are her clothes in the living room? They'll need to be bagged and checked for trace evidence."

Sheriff Tickman shook his head no. "I didn't find any clothes down here. I did find a skimpy little robe on a chair in the living room. I've bagged it, but I haven't found the clothes she was wearing."

"Do you think whoever killed her took them?"

"Either that or she was only wearing the robe. You think she was murdered, then?"

"There's some bruising around her neck. It's a good possibility. I'd consider this entire house a crime scene for now, if I were you."

"Ya, I guess. But I have an idea we're going to find a lot of fingerprints from a lot of different people."

"You mean a lot of different men, don't you?" Dr. Galante asked.

The sheriff was quiet, thinking about his reply. "So, you've heard the rumors, too?"

"I've heard talk. I never paid much attention to it, though. I figured it was just a lot of gossip."

"Maybe. I guess we'll find out, won't we?"

Dr. Galante closed his medical bag. "Are you done with her? I'm ready to take her."

Sheriff Tickman shook his head no. "I need a few more pictures before you move the body, Doc."

"I already took pictures," the doctor said.

"Ya, I know you did. But I want a few more shots from a different angle. Give me a minute, will you?" the sheriff asked.

The coroner stepped back, giving Sheriff Tickman room. "I'll put my stuff in the van. Let me know when you're done."

Sheriff Tickman watched while Marjorie Finnegan's body was loaded into the coroner's van. He waved goodbye as Dr. Galante drove off and walked back into the house. He took a seat across from Michael Finnegan and studied the man. His eyes were puffy and red, but he had finally stopped crying. Michael reached for a tissue and blew his nose.

Finnegan looked up at the sheriff. "I'm sorry. I just don't seem to be able to pull myself together. I just can't believe Marg is gone."

"I am truly sorry for your loss, Michael. It's a terrible thing. Do you think you could answer some questions now?"

Michael looked confused. "Questions? About what? I came home and found her on the dining room floor and called you. That's all I know."

"You said you didn't touch her. Is that right?"

Michael closed his eyes and sighed. "Not exactly. I felt for a pulse. When I didn't find one, I called you."

"I see. Why didn't you call for an ambulance before you called me?"

"I don't understand the question. She was dead. Why would I call for an ambulance?" Michael asked.

"How could you be so sure she was dead?"

"She wasn't breathing, that's how. Plus, she felt kinda cool. And, her lips...." Michael looked away. "I just knew she was dead."

"I need to go over everything that Marjorie had planned for today. Was she expecting any visitors? Maybe, some friends were coming over?"

"She didn't mention anything this morning. I don't know what she had planned."

"Tell me what you did today. Did you come home during the day for any reason? Have you seen anyone hanging around outside the house recently?"

"No. Nothing like that. I was at work all day. It was just like any other morning. I had breakfast, kissed her goodbye, and left for work. I got home around six-thirty. It was just another routine day. At least it was until I got home and found her."

"So, as far as you know, she wasn't planning on going anywhere?" Sheriff Tickman asked.

"I don't think so. At least, she didn't mention it."

"Michael, I need to know if any of her clothes are missing."

Michael's head jerked up and he stared at the sheriff. "You think somebody stole her clothes? That's ridiculous."

"We didn't find the clothes she was wearing. I can only assume that her assailant took them with him when he left."

"I need a drink." Michael suddenly stood up and headed towards the kitchen.

"Wait," the sheriff called out.

Michael stopped and looked back at him. "What?"

"You need to stay in here. We haven't finished going over the kitchen yet."

"Then, tell one of your cops to bring me a glass and the bottle that's in the cabinet above the sink. I need a drink," he declared in a loud voice. He glared at the sheriff, then, lowered his eyes. "I'm sorry. Please. I could really use a drink right now."

"Sit down, Michael. I'll get it for you."

"Thank you," Michael said, softly.

Michael downed his drink in one swallow. "I had breakfast at about 6:30. Marg didn't eat with me. She was doing the dishes while I ate." He hesitated. "We joked around a little and I left," he finally said. "She didn't mention what her plans were for the day."

"What do you mean you joked around a little?" the sheriff inquired.

"We played around. You know."

"You made love?" the sheriff asked.

Michael's cheeks turned red. "Yes, we made love."

"Here? Downstairs?"

Michael stared at him. "Yes, down here. On the kitchen table, if you must know."

"Did you do that often? On the table, I mean."

Michael looked away. "Sheriff," he finally said, "I figure we made love on every surface in this house at one time or another. Marjorie was a very sexual person, as am I."

"I see."

"There's a good possibility that Marjorie wasn't dressed when she was attacked. That may be why you didn't find any clothes down here," Michael told him.

Sheriff Tickman looked up from his notebook, a surprised look on his face. "Why would you think that?"

"It's a feeling I have. She enjoyed being nude. The fewer clothes she had to wear, the better. She was naked when I left the house this morning. Perhaps, she hadn't had time to get dressed before she was attacked."

"Perhaps," Sheriff Tickman said. "But the coroner thinks she died somewhere between three-thirty and five this afternoon. He'll know more after the autopsy, but that's his best estimate for now."

"Autopsy? He's going to cut her open? No! I won't allow it."

"I'm sorry, Michael, but we have to know the exact cause of death. An autopsy is required any time there is a suspicious death."

Finnegan handed his glass to the sheriff. "Another one, please."

"Sorry. I can't do that until I'm finished questioning you."

"Well, I'm done talking and I'd like you to leave. I've told you everything I know. I'd like to be alone now."

"Again, I'm sorry. You can't stay here tonight. We should be done here tomorrow sometime, but we need to go through the entire house before you can stay here again. Do you have a place where you can sleep tonight? Perhaps, at a friend's house?"

"Don't you need a search warrant for that, Sheriff?" Michael asked, obviously upset.

"No. Your wife was killed here today. We don't need one."

Michael stood up and stared at the sheriff. "This isn't right."

"I know you're upset and I don't blame you. But we need your help, Michael. We need you to work with us to find the person who did this."

"Well, then, is it all right if I get some personal

items and a change of clothes before I leave?" he asked.

"Of course. I'll have Deputy Fitzgerald go with you while you get what you need," the Sheriff replied.

"Shaun? I didn't know he was here."

"You know Shaun?" the Sheriff asked him.

"We grew up together." Michael looked at the sheriff and sighed. "I'm sorry, I'm not myself. I'll stay at a motel tonight."

"Shaun," the sheriff yelled. "Get in here." He glanced over at Michael. "I'll want to talk to you tomorrow morning. Please, meet me at the station around nine."

"More questions?" Michael declared. "I've already told you everything I know."

"Perhaps, but I still want to see you at nine o'clock. Got it?"

<u>Three</u>

Sheriff Tickman was seated at a large conference table with Deputy Shaun Fitzgerald, Officer Lawrence Larson, Officer Fred Nettle, Officer Laura Edwards, and Sally Thompson. Sally, one of the two office employees, was there to record the meeting.

"The majority of the Finnegan's neighbors are elderly and have lived in that sub-division for years. As they die off or move into assisted living facilities, younger couples are moving in. But, as we all know, people are living longer than ever these days, so there are still a lot of gray heads living there," Sally Thompson informed the group.

"Gray heads, Sally?" the sheriff said, grinning.

Sally shrugged.

"All right. Let's go over what we know so far," Sheriff Tickman said. "Marjorie Finnegan, age 31, was found dead by her husband at approximately 6:30 last night. He states that she was well and alive when he left for work in the morning. He was unaware of any plans she had for the day, including any visitors."

"How did he seem to you when you spoke with him?" Officer Nettle asked.

"I didn't get much out of him at first. He finally settled down a little, but he seemed genuinely upset. He says he was in Palatine all day. Laura, I want you to check that out. Talk to his secretary and be sure he is telling the truth."

"Will do," Officer Edwards said.

"You know, Palatine isn't that far. He could have

come home during his lunch hour," Officer Larson stated.

"True, but Doc Galante thinks she was killed a few hours after that," Tickman replied. He made a few notes in a notebook and looked up. "Did any of you get anything useful from the neighbors you talked to last night?" He looked over at Deputy Fitzgerald and grinned. "I heard you had the door slammed in your face. Made an old man mad, did you?"

Fitzgerald smiled. "I thought the old fart was gonna take a swing at me. Man, he was really upset."

"Well, we're going to canvas the rest of the neighborhood today. We need to find someone who saw something. After all, what else do these people have to do all day except look out the window and watch their neighbors?"

"Really, Sheriff? Some of these old people could run rings around you," Officer Edwards commented.

"I highly doubt it," he said, laughing. "Did anyone but Larry get any information?"

He waited a few seconds for someone to respond. "Nothing, huh? Okay, then. Larry, tell us what you found out from Mrs. McDonald?"

Officer Larson opened his notebook, flipped the pages until he came to what he was looking for, and smiled. "According to Mrs. McDonald, Marjorie Finnegan was a harlot. Her words, not mine."

"What the hell is a harlot?" Officer Nettle, the youngest cop on the force, asked.

"A prostitute, whore, hussy, loose woman, hooker, slut. Take your pick. Mrs. McDonald used them all during our conversation. In other words,

17

Fred, according to Mrs. McDonald, Marjorie Finnegan was an extremely promiscuous woman."

"Go on," Sheriff Tickman said.

"It seems that the mailman delivered more than the mail. Mrs. McDonald watched him enter the Finnegan's house on many occasions, stay five or ten minutes, and leave. The same thing went on with the UPS driver. Mrs. McDonald said there were days he went to the door without carrying any packages."

"And, did she also see him go inside the house?" Tickman asked.

"On numerous occasions. And, although it was hard to see through the Finnegans' screen door - the screen being so dark and all - she was pretty sure that Mrs. Finnegan was usually in a robe when she answered the door."

"Holy crap," Officer Nettle said. "Who knew this was going on right here in our own town."

"Don't jump to conclusions, Officer," Sheriff Tickman said. "We don't know if any of this is true."

"Well," Officer Larson continued, "Mrs. McDonald certainly believes it. She also said that Mrs. Finnegan occasionally had other men visitors during the day. She said they never stayed very long. Perhaps, fifteen minutes or so. Sometimes, a little longer."

"What about yesterday, Larry? Did she see anyone go into the house yesterday?" Sheriff Tickman inquired.

"She did," Officer Larson told him. "In fact, she saw several people." He glanced down at his notes.

"Well?" Tickman said loudly, after a few seconds of silence. "Who did she see?"

"The mailman and the UPS driver," Larson told the Sheriff, as he flipped a page in his notebook. "Oh, ya. And, the paperboy," he said, looking up at the sheriff."

Sheriff Tickman turned to Sally. "Sally, I need you to. . . "

"I'm on it," Sally replied. "I'll get their names."

"What time was the paperboy there?" the Sheriff asked.

"She wasn't sure. It was in the afternoon, though."

"Well, I doubt it was the paper boy who killed her, so that leaves the mailman and the UPS driver," the sheriff said. "What about the other men Mrs. McDonald said she occasionally saw go into the house? Do you think she could describe them?" he asked Officer Larson.

"I'm not sure, but I'll check with her. I think she has pretty good vision. Most old people can see better than I can. After they get that cataract surgery, their vision is usually 20/20," Larson replied.

"Okay, that's it for now. It's almost nine and I need to talk to Michael Finnegan. You guys get out there and find someone who might know something. Talk to all their neighbors. If you see kids, talk to them, too. Kids usually don't miss anything.

<u>Four</u>

When he walked into the room, the first thing that Sheriff Tickman observed was that Michael Finnegan looked like hell. His eyes were bloodshot, his hair was a mess, and his clothes looked like he had slept in them.

"How are you doing, Michael?" Tickman asked.

Finnegan looked up and gave him a weak smile. "I feel worse than I look, and I look like shit. You figure it out," he said.

"I've always found that you can't drink your troubles away," Tickman told him. "They may disappear for a while, but when you sober up, they're still there. It seems that all you've accomplished is to give yourself one hell of a headache."

"I guess."

"Are you feeling well enough to answer a few questions?"

"You wouldn't happen to have a couple of aspirins, would you? And, maybe a cup of strong, black coffee?"

Tickman grinned. "I think we just might be able to provide that." He turned and walked over to the open door. "Sally, we need some aspirin and a cup of black coffee in here," he yelled.

Michael looked up at him. "Thanks."

Sheriff Tickman sat down across the table from Finnegan, laid a pad of paper in front of him, took out his pen, and sighed. "Ready?"

"As ready as I'll ever be," Finnegan replied.

"Walk me through your day again," Tickman said.

"All right. It's just like I told you last night. I left the house a little after seven, was at work all day, and got home around six-thirty. I found Marg lying on the floor in the dining room and I called 911."

"I noticed your car was in the driveway. How did you enter your house?"

"I came in through the back door like I usually do."

"Do you always use the back door?" the Sheriff asked.

"Usually. Except in the winter. Then, I use the entrance into the kitchen from the door in the garage."

"Why don't you park in the garage the rest of the time?"

"Too much crap in there. I'm terrible about putting things away. I always make sure that there's room for Margie's car, though. She always puts her car in the garage."

"Was the garage door closed when you left for work yesterday?"

Michael thought for a few seconds, then shook his head yes. "It was closed. I know what you're thinking. That someone could have come into the house through the garage. The garage door was shut."

"You're sure?" Tickman asked.

"I'm sure."

"So, you said you were at your office the entire day," the sheriff stated. "Did you leave at any time? Were there any appointments you went to? Maybe you went to the bank? Where did you go for lunch?"

"Sheriff, I didn't jump in my car, rush home, and kill my wife over my lunch hour."

"I have to ask, Michael. Sorry."

"Usually, my clients come to me. So, no, I didn't leave for any appointments during the day."

"You're a travel agent, right?"

"Right."

"Okay," Sheriff Tickman said. "Did you go out for lunch?"

Michael hesitated a second before answering. "I did. I left the office for about an hour, between 12:30 and 1:30."

"Where did you go?" Tickman asked.

"I picked up a burger at Wendy's, drove to Centennial Park, sat on a bench, and watched the ducks while I ate my lunch."

"Were you with anyone?"

"No. I was alone. After I finished my lunch, I made a few phone calls and I went back to the office."

Sheriff Tickman made some notes on his pad and sat back. "Those aspirin kicking in yet?" he asked Michael.

Michael Finnegan shook his head no. "Not really. I'm such an idiot. I really overdid it last night. It's gonna take the rest of the day before I start to feel human again."

"Who did you call?" the sheriff inquired.

"What?" Finnegan looked at him confused.

"You said you made some phone calls. Who did you call?"

"Oh. Right. I called and made an appointment to have my car serviced." Finnegan was quiet for a few

22

seconds. "I called Marg, too."

"You talked to your wife? What time was that?"

"I called her, but she didn't answer. I figured she was shopping or something."

"Time?" the sheriff asked again.

Michael pulled out his phone and checked his call log. "It was 1:10 when I called her."

The Sheriff glanced over at the open door and noticed Sally Thompson standing there looking at him. "Something you need, Sally?" he asked.

She handed him a slip of paper. "Sorry to bother you. I thought you should see this."

Sheriff Tickman read the note. "I'll be there in a minute," he told her. He looked over at Finnegan. "Michael, I need to make a fast phone call. I'll be right back."

"Fine with me," Finnegan replied, as he laid his head on the table and closed his eyes.

"Coffee?" Sally asked her boss.

"God, no. I've had enough for today. Did Dr. Galante say what he wanted?"

"No. He just said he would be in the office until noon and you should call him. After that, he won't be available until Monday."

"Thanks. Get him on the line, will you? I'll be in my office."

Sheriff Tickman hung up the phone and walked into the bullpen. Most of the desks were empty. His men were out canvassing the Finnegan's neighborhood, hoping to find some clue that would lead them to who killed Marjorie Finnegan. He took a deep breath, let it out, and walked back to the interview room to continue his conversation with Finnegan.

"Shit," he muttered to himself. The man was sound asleep, spittle running down the side of his chin onto the table.

"Michael," he said loudly. "Wake up."

Michael slowly lifted his head and looked up at the sheriff. "Just how friggin' tall are you?" he asked.

"Wake up. I need to finish taking your statement."

Michael sat up and wiped his chin with the back of his hand. "Sorry, about that."

"Can anyone confirm that you were in the park between 12:30 and 1:30?" the sheriff asked bluntly, starting to get impatient with Michael.

"I'm not sure. I mean, like, I saw a lot of people there, but I don't know if they'd remember me or not."

"We talked to your secretary, Michael. She said that you left the office at 12:15 and didn't get back until 1:30. That's an hour and fifteen minutes. It takes about twenty minutes to drive from Palatine to Cary. You had plenty of time to drive home, kill your wife, and be back to work by 1:30."

Michael's head jerked up and he stared at the Sheriff. "You think I killed her? Well, you're wrong. I loved her. There's no way I would ever hurt Margie."

"I just got the prelim from the coroner. The blood tests show that she had traces of ecstasy in her blood."

Michael looked shocked. "There's got to be a mistake. Margie doesn't ... Margie didn't use drugs."

"No mistake. He found marijuana, too." Sheriff Tickman sat back in his chair and stared at Michael.

Michael looked at him and then looked away. "She didn't use drugs."

"If I take a sample of your blood right now, will I find traces of ecstasy?"

Michael didn't answer him.

Tickman waited. "Think about it, Michael. I'll be right back." He stood up and left the room.

Ten minutes later Sheriff Tickman was once again seated across from Michael Finnegan. "Anything you want to tell me?" he asked Michael.

"We do a little ecstasy now and then. You know how it is. It perks up the sex a little, makes it better."

"No, I don't know how it is. Did you take ecstasy Thursday night?"

"We did."

"How often do you smoke pot?" the Sheriff asked.

"I don't smoke that often. I think Marg smokes more - did smoke more than me."

"So, she did do drugs. What else have you been lying to me about, Michael?"

"Nothing. I swear to God, Sheriff. Everything I've told you is the truth, except for the drugs part."

"You do know that ecstasy is an illegal substance, don't you? You just admitted to breaking the law."

Michael looked indignant. "My wife's killer is out there and you want to arrest me for doing a little E? What the hell? I think you need to get your priorities straight, Sheriff," he said, raising his voice. "I don't feel well and I'd like to leave, if you don't mind. Unless you plan on arresting me, in which case I'd like to call an attorney."

Sheriff Tickman stood and picked up his pad of paper. He gave Michael an icy stare. "We're done for now. Just don't leave town, Michael. I'm going to need to talk to you again."

"If you want to speak to me again, call my attorney. I'm done here."

Michael Finnegan stood and started to leave the room.

"Michael," Tickman called out.

Michael turned and looked at him. "What now?"

"I mean it. Don't plan any trips."

"I don't intend to, Sheriff. I have a wife to bury. Remember?"

Five

"You have a lovely home, Mrs. Montgomery. Have you lived here for a long time?" Officer Laura Edwards asked.

"Yes, I have. Henry and I bought this house when it was brand new. We hadn't been married very long at that time. It was a struggle, but we managed and we paid it off years ago. He died in 1999, so it's just me now."

"I'm sorry for your loss." She took a sip from her cup. Laura smiled at the elderly woman. "This is a very good cup of tea. Do you use a special brand?"

"Oh, my, no. It's just regular old tea. The secret is in the way you brew it."

"Well, whatever you do, it works."

"It's so sad about Marjorie Finnegan. She seemed like such a friendly lady."

Officer Edwards looked over at her. "Did you know her well?"

"Not really. They haven't lived here that long. She always said hello when I saw her and one time, when I had the flu, she brought me some soup. It was very good if I remember correctly."

"Do you remember when they moved in?"

"Of course. It will be two years in December. They moved in right before Christmas," Mrs. Montgomery told her.

"I understand she didn't work," Officer Edwards stated. "Did she have a lot of visitors?"

"I can't say," Sarah Montgomery replied. "My eyesight isn't as good as it used to be and I don't spend a lot of time spying on my neighbors."

"Of course not. I didn't mean to imply that you did. I just wondered if you ever saw anything that might help us."

"Well, for one thing, I think she spent a lot of money."

"Really? Why do you think that?" Officer Edwards asked.

"She was always getting packages delivered. Emma said she was probably buying a lot of stuff on the net. Do you know what that is?"

"I do. I sometimes buy things on Amazon when I can't find what I want in the stores," Officer Edwards told her.

Mrs. Montgomery gave her a strange look. "You buy things from the Amazon? What do you buy from down there that you can't get here in the United States?"

Officer Edwards smiled. "Amazon is a website. It's a place on the internet, like a store, that sells things. I didn't mean the Amazon in South America."

Mrs. Montgomery looked confused. "I don't know how you keep up with all the changes going on in this world. Emma got a cell phone that she carries with her. Do you have one of those, too?"

"I do have one. But, before, when you said Marjorie Finnegan got a lot of packages, did you mean she got a lot of packages that were delivered by UPS?"

"Yes. Sometimes Emma and I joked about how long the driver stayed in her house when he delivered them. We figured he was doing more than helping her open those packages."

Officer Edwards smiled. "You figured a little hanky panky was going on, did you?

Sarah Montgomery looked Officer Edwards straight in her eyes. "Well, what would you think? And, then there's the mailman. Everyone else gets their mail delivered to their mailboxes out on the street. We have to walk out to our boxes to get our mail. Not Marjorie. She got hers delivered right to her front door and sometimes right into her house. What was so special about her, I'd like to know."

"You saw the mailman go into her house? That does seem unusual."

"Well, I can't prove anything," Mrs. Montgomery declared. "But Emma and I had our suspicions."

"Do you recall if the UPS driver or the mailman were in her house on Friday?"

"They both were. I didn't see them, but Emma told me that they were. Although, she did say that the mailman left her house after just a few minutes. Emma said that the UPS driver stayed longer, though." She looked up at Officer Edwards. "What else could have been going on, Officer? She had to be fucking them. Right?"

Officer Edwards's head jerked up in surprise, and she fought to stifle a laugh. Sarah Montgomery was looking at her, a serious look on her face, waiting for her to answer.

"Mrs. Montgomery, I . . ." Edwards lost it, and started to laugh.

"Please, call me Sarah."

Officer Edwards pulled herself together and smiled at the woman. "Sorry about that. I wasn't expecting you to say that. May I ask how old you are?"

"Why, of course. I'm going to be seventy-seven in October."

"Well, I never would have guessed it. You look a lot younger."

"Thank you, dear."

"So, Mrs. . ." Officer Edwards caught herself. "So, Sarah, Emma told you about the UPS driver and the mailman being there on Friday but you didn't see them for yourself. Is that correct?"

"It is. But I've seen them myself on many occasions, so I believe her."

"Did you see anyone there on Friday?" Edwards asked, emphasizing the word you.

"You mean did I see any people myself?" Sarah Montgomery said, quietly, almost to herself. Suddenly, she smiled. "Of course, I did. Lyle Sleeter was there. He's our paperboy and he collects on Fridays. I saw him there."

"Do you remember what time it was when you saw him?"

"I believe I do," Sarah Montgomery replied. "He was there between 2:30 and 3:00. I remember because that's when I went out to get my mail."

"Very good. Thank you."

"He was there at 4:30, too," Mrs. Montgomery added.

Officer Edwards looked up from her pad. "He was there twice?"

"Well, he didn't go in the first time. I know he stood there for a little while, waiting for Marjorie to answer the door. Finally, he just turned around and left."

"But he came back?" Officer Edwards inquired.

"Oh, my, yes. He came back at 4:30. She must have answered the door because he went in the house."

"Did you see what time he left?"

"No. I was watching my soaps. It couldn't have been long, though. I mean, how long does it take to collect a little money?"

Officer Edwards finished her cup of tea and set the cup back on the saucer. "Is there anything else you can think of that might help us?"

Sarah Montgomery gave her a motherly smile and shook her head no. "You have a very dangerous job, you know," she said to Edwards. "You need to be careful."

Officer Edwards smiled back at her. "I will. Thank you. I guess that's it then," she said, as she stood up. "If you think of anything else, please give me a call." She reached into her pocket, pulled out her card, and handed it to Mrs. Montgomery.

"Did Emma tell you about the car?" she asked, as Officer Edwards headed towards the door.

Edwards turned and look at her. "I'm sorry. What car?"

"There was a car parked in front of the Finnegan's house for a while on Friday afternoon."

"Did you see the car or did Emma tell you about it?" Edwards asked her.

"Oh, no. I saw it. We both did. It was a gray car and a woman was driving it. I didn't see her get out of the car, though. It's probably nothing."

"Did you get a good look at the woman?"

"Not really. She had long blond hair. I couldn't see her face. I just saw the top of her head. She was looking down. I guess she might have been checking something on her cell phone. Emma does that a lot, although I don't know why. She never finds anything." She looked up and smiled. "That's about all I remember."

"Do you know what kind of a car it was?" Officer Edwards asked.

"I'm sorry. I don't. My husband would know. He knew every car on the road. All I remember is that it was gray. Or, silver. It might have been silver. And, it had four doors. It was a regular car, not those big ones that people drive these days."

"You mean an SUV?"

"Yes. It wasn't one of those. It was smaller."

Do you recall what the license plate looked like?"

Mrs. Montgomery closed her eyes and thought for a few seconds. "It was white," she finally declared.

"White," Edwards repeated. She jotted the information in her notepad and smiled at Mrs. Montgomery. "You've been a great help," she told the elderly woman. "Thank you, and thanks for a great cup of tea."

"Stop by any time, dearie. And, be careful out there, you hear."

<u>Six</u>

Officer Edwards had her phone out of her pocket before she made it to her squad car. She called Sheriff Tickman, who answered on the first ring.

"I think we should bring Lyle Sleeter in for questioning," she told him. "Like right now, Sheriff," she added.

"Who is Lyle Sleeter?"

"He's the Finnegan's paper boy. I just finished talking with Sarah Montgomery, one of the neighbors. She's quite the lady, by the way. Anyway, she mentioned that she saw the Sleeter boy at the Finnegan house around 2:30 or so and again at 4:30. He might be the last person who talked to Marjorie before she was killed."

"Do you know where he lives?" the sheriff asked her.

"Over on Margaret Terrace. I'm not sure of the house number, but I know which house it is."

"Go pick him up," Sheriff Tickman said. "Bring him in now."

"He's a minor, you know," Officer Edwards reminded the Sheriff.

"We're just talking to him, not arresting him."

"Right," Edwards replied. "I'm not far from there. I'll see if he's home."

"Just find him," the sheriff said.

Thirty minutes later, Lyle Sleeter was sitting in Interview Room Two, checking his phone for messages.

He put the phone in his pocket when he heard the door open and sat up straight in his chair.

"Hey, Lyle, how's it going?" Sheriff Tickman asked as he entered the room.

Lyle looked up at him and gave him a nervous smile. "Fine, I guess," he answered. "Why am I here? That lady cop wouldn't tell me anything."

"There's nothing to worry about. I just need to ask you a couple of questions."

"This is about Mrs. Finnegan, isn't it?" Lyle asked.

"It is. I understand you saw her yesterday. Is that correct?"

Lyle looked away, not answering the Sheriff.

"Is that right?" the Sheriff asked again.

"I didn't really see her. I was there to collect for the paper, but she didn't answer the door."

The sheriff sat back in his chair and studied the young man. "How old are you, Lyle?"

"Why do you need to know that?" Lyle replied defensively.

"Just wondering, is all."

"I'm fifteen."

The sheriff looked surprised. "Really? I thought you were older than that. You sure look older. You're pretty tall, too."

Lyle grinned. "Not as tall as you, Sheriff. You're really tall."

The sheriff smiled. "I got a second growth spurt after I went away to college. I was already about six-two when I got out of high school and everyone figured I had quit growing."

"How tall are you now?" Lyle inquired.

"Six feet seven inches," the sheriff told him.

"Wow! You should have been a basketball player."

"I thought about it, but I wasn't good enough. You still have some growing to do. I figure you'll probably hit at least six-two before you quit growing."

"I guess I could. I'm five-eleven now," Lyle said,

"Well, you could easily pass for eighteen or nineteen."

"That's what my mom always says."

"You're on the football team, aren't you?" the sheriff inquired.

Lyle grinned. "Sure am. I'm on the varsity team even though I'm only a sophomore."

"I thought you looked familiar. You're in the same grade as my daughter, Valerie. I've seen you play. You're good."

"Thanks," Lyle said.

"Can I get you something to drink?"

Lyle slouched in the chair, an indication that he was becoming more comfortable. "Na. Maybe later."

"Tell me what you did yesterday. Mostly, what you did in the afternoon."

"I was collecting money from the people on my paper route."

"Are the Finnegans customers of yours?"

"Yah," Lyle answered.

"Do you remember what time it was when you were at the Finnegan's house?"

Lyle Sleeter pursed his lips and rolled his eyes up towards the ceiling, thinking about his answer.

After a few seconds, he smiled and said, "It was quarter to three. At least, I'm pretty sure it was."

"And, was Mrs. Finnegan home?"

Lyle shook his head no.

"She wasn't home or she didn't answer the door?"

Lyle looked away, his cheeks turning red.

"Which is it, Lyle? I need you to answer me," the sheriff told him.

"She didn't answer the door."

"So, she was home?"

"I guess," Lyle muttered.

"But she didn't answer the door?"

"No," Lyle replied.

"Did she see you at the door?"

"I think so."

"Well, that's kind of strange, don't you think? If she was home, and she saw you standing on the porch, why didn't she answer the door?"

Lyle's only response was to look down at the floor.

"Well?" the sheriff said. "I'm waiting for your answer.

Lyle looked at the sheriff, an angry look on his face. "Because she wasn't alone. Okay?" he said loudly. "She was with someone."

"Did you see the person she was with?" the sheriff asked.

"Only his back. I only saw his back. Marjorie was looking at me. I couldn't see the other person's face, but it was the man who drives the UPS truck."

"How do you know if you couldn't see his face?"

Tickman asked.

"Because his truck was parked out front. Okay?" Lyle looked away. "I don't want to talk about this anymore."

"I'm sorry, Lyle. I know this is hard for you. I only have a couple more questions."

"I thought she was a nice lady," Lyle suddenly shouted. "She always gave me a tip when I collected my money and she told me to call her Marjorie. I really..."

Sheriff Tickman waited. "You really what, Lyle? Tell me what you were going to say."

"She told me that she liked me and that she thought I was special." He looked at the sheriff. "She lied to me."

"Why do you think she lied?" the Sheriff asked him.

"I thought I was the only one who was special. That's what she told me. But he was special, too."

"The man she was with?" Tickman asked softly.

"She was naked with him and he was touching her. I saw him and she knew I was watching her. She smiled at me. While he was doing things to her, she smiled at me."

"I'm sorry you had to see that, Lyle," the sheriff said. "What did you do after you saw her and the UPS man?"

Tears started rolling down Lyle's cheeks. He looked away from the sheriff. "Can I get something to drink now?" he asked.

"In a minute. First, tell me what you did."

"I left."

"You didn't say anything or go into her house?"

Lyle looked up at him, surprised at his question. "No. I just left. I didn't want to see her with him anymore. Can I go now?"

"Just a couple more questions. Was the man dressed or naked? I'm sorry to ask, Lyle, but I need to know."

"He had his shirt on."

"What about his pants?"

Lyle looked down at his hands and shook his head no.

"No pants?"

"No. No pants," Lyle said.

"Were they having sex?"

"I said I don't want to talk about this anymore," Lyle told him.

Sheriff Tickman stood. "I have water, apple juice, or Coke. What can I get you?"

"Coke, please."

Sheriff Tickman walked out of the room into the bullpen. He stood there, trying to digest what Lyle had just told him. If he had understood him correctly, Marjorie Finnegan had been having sex with a fifteen-year-old boy.

Seven

"Can I call my mom?" Lyle asked the sheriff.

"Ms. Thompson just called her and told her you were here talking to me."

"Is she coming to get me?"

"No. We told her we would give you a ride home when we're done interviewing you."

Lyle looked concerned. "She didn't want to come and get me? Why wouldn't she want to come and pick me up?"

"She did, but Ms. Thompson told her not to bother. She told your mom that we'd probably have you home by lunchtime," Sheriff Tickman told him, trying to placate him.

"Is that for me?" Lyle asked, looking at the can of Coke the sheriff was holding.

"It sure is," the Tickman replied, handing him the beverage. He watched while Lyle took a long swallow, and, then, burped. He grinned. "Coke always makes me do that, too."

Lyle smiled back. "Sorry,"

"Can you think of anything else that might help us? Did you see anyone else there yesterday?"

Lyle shook his head no. "Nope. After I left her house, I finished collecting from my other customers and went home."

"Did you see Mrs. Finnegan again that day?"

Lyle glanced over at him, then, looked away. "No," he finally muttered.

"I'm sorry. I didn't hear that," the sheriff said.

"No. I didn't see her again," Lyle said loudly.

"Well, I thought maybe you went back later to collect the money she owed you," the sheriff told him.

"Well, I didn't. Can I get that ride home now?"

"Lyle, I want you to think about this long and hard before you answer me. Did you see Mrs. Finnegan again?"

"I just told you – no!" Lyle said loudly.

"Think again," the sheriff said softly. "Lying to a police officer is a crime, you know."

Lyle jumped as the noise of his cell phone ringing started him. He started to reach for it, then, looked up at the Sheriff. "Can I answer it?"

"No, you can't. Let it go to voice mail."

A few moments later, there was a ding, indicating that a message had been left on Lyle's phone.

"Turn it off, will you?" the sheriff asked him. He waited while Lyle took the phone out of his back pocket and turned it off.

Lyle looked up at the sheriff. "Now, can I go home?"

"No, you can't. Give me your phone."

Lyle gave him a dirty look. "No way. I'm not giving you my phone."

"Just give it to me." The sheriff held out his hand and waited.

Lyle didn't move.

"Now!" the sheriff yelled.

Lyle laid his phone on the table and pushed it over to the Sheriff.

"I'll be right back," Sheriff Tickman said, as he

grabbed the phone and walked out of the room.

A few minutes later, the sheriff was back in the interview room. "All right, son. Let me tell you what I know for sure," he said, watching the expression on Lyle's face. "You went back to Mrs. Finnegan's house a couple of hours later. You went..."

"No, I didn't," Lyle yelled, interrupting the sheriff.

"I have two witnesses that say you did. You were there at 4:30. Now, stop lying to me."

"I want an attorney," Lyle said angrily.

"You watch too many movies. I haven't arrested you for anything and you don't need an attorney. Now, did you go back to Mrs. Finnegan's house around 4:30?"

Lyle looked up at the ceiling. "I might have," he said, not looking at Sheriff Tickman.

"Not might have. You did. You were angry with her. Almost two hours had gone by and you were furious at what you had seen. You went back to confront her and this time she was alone, so she let you in. You argued with her and she laughed at you. Maybe, she called you a little boy trying to be a big man."

Lyle didn't say a word. He just stared at the sheriff, a shocked expression on his face. He shook his head no. "I didn't . . ."

"All this time, here you are, thinking you're the only one she's spending her time with, making love to," the sheriff continued. "And, then, you find out that she's messing around with the UPS driver. You're

41

upset and you want her to reassure you that she still wants you. You want to have it out with her. She laughs at you and tells you to grow up. You figure if you can't have her, no one will. You grab her and she fights back. Maybe, she hits you and tells you to get out of her house. Whatever! You're so mad you can't see straight."

"No!" Lyle cried out. "I didn't...."

"You throw her down on the floor and straddle her and, then, Lyle, you choke the life out of her body. You probably didn't mean to do it, but you're in a jealous rage and you can't stop yourself. This is what happened, isn't it? Did you rape her, too? You might as well tell me now, Lyle, because the autopsy will show if she was raped by you."

"You're wrong, Sheriff. I didn't."

"I know you did it, Lyle. You were the last person to see her alive. When you left her house, she was dead. It had to be you." He looked at Lyle, whose face had turned white. "That's what happened, isn't it?"

"No. Why are you making all this stuff up? I didn't hurt her. She was dead when I got there," he cried out.

"If she was dead when you got there, why didn't you call for help? Listen to me, Lyle. We found the picture you took of her on your phone. It's time-stamped at 4:45. That's fifteen minutes after you got there. That gives you plenty of time to kill and rape her."

Lyle started sobbing. "No! You're wrong," he told the sheriff.

"Why did you take that picture if you didn't kill

42

her? You wanted a memento – a reminder of what you had done, didn't you?"

"No. I didn't kill her." Tears rolled down his cheeks. He moaned and looked down at his wet pants.

"Don't worry," the sheriff said. "I'll tell your mom to bring you some clean clothes when she comes to see you."

"I didn't do it, Sheriff. I loved her. I wouldn't hurt her."

"Well, young man, I think you did and I am arresting you for her murder."

"No," Lyle cried. "She was dead when I got there."

"I'm sorry, but I don't believe you," Sheriff Tickman said and proceeded to Mirandize him.

"I'm not telling you how to do your job, Tic, but don't you think you should have waited before arresting the kid? Where's your evidence?"

Sheriff Tickman looked at his deputy. "He took a picture of her dead body, for god's sake. He did it."

"I'm not so sure," Deputy Fitzgerald said.

"She was alive when he got there at 4:30. She answered the door."

"Did anyone see her answer the door? Or, maybe he got there a little later," Fitzgerald commented.

"It doesn't make any difference. She was dead when her husband got home around 6:30 or so. Doc Galante said she'd been dead a couple of hours. No one else was there. It has to be him. He'd been having sex with her, for god's sake. He was jealous. He couldn't control his temper. He killed her. End of story."

"Maybe," the deputy replied. "But it would sure help if you had some evidence. Like DNA or something."

"I'll bet you anything that Doc will find something. Anyway, until I know I'm wrong, he's staying right where he is."

"Tic, we haven't even interviewed Charlie Peters or Dan Samuels yet. Don't you think we should at least talk to them?"

Sheriff Tickman shook his head yes in agreement. "Of course, we should. We need to get statements from everyone. But I'm telling you, Shaun, that kid is guilty as sin."

Eight

Late Saturday afternoon, Deputy Shaun Fitzgerald watched as Charlie Peters strutted out of Interview Room One and headed towards the exit. He was the last person to be interviewed in the Finnegan murder case. Fitzgerald turned his chair back towards his desk and tried to concentrate on his paperwork.

As promised, Sheriff Tickman had interviewed Charlie Peters, and Dan Samuels - the mailman and the UPS driver who had been seen entering the Finnegan house on the day of the murder.

Charlie Peters admitted that he occasionally stepped into the Finnegan house for a quickie with Marjorie Finnegan, as did Dan Samuels. Peters was crossed off as a suspect, as Dan Samuels had been in the house after Peters and, obviously, Marjorie had still been alive.

However, there was no direct evidence to connect Samuels to her death and he swore she was still very much alive when he had left. Sheriff Tickman also crossed him off the list.

Except for Emma McDonald and Sarah Montgomery, no one else in the neighborhood had admitted to seeing anything unusual the day that Marjorie Finnegan was murdered. That left the Sleeter boy as the prime suspect, and Sheriff Tickman had the boy behind bars.

"Where's my son?"

Deputy Fitzgerald looked up and watched as an extremely good-looking woman entered the police

45

station. She stopped walking and glanced around the room. Her eyes settled on Fitzgerald and she headed towards his desk.

Officer Nettle jumped out of his chair and interrupted her progress. He held out his hand, indicating that she should stop. "Sorry, ma'am. You can't be back here."

"Get the hell out of my way," she yelled. "I want to see my son. Now!"

Nettle glanced over at Fitzgerald, not sure what to do.

Deputy Fitzgerald stood and walked over to the woman. "Is there something I can help you with?" he asked her.

"Where's my boy? Where's Lyle? I want to see him right now."

"Mrs. Sleeter?" Fitzgerald asked.

"Where is he? Where's Lyle?"

"I'm sorry, Mrs. Sleeter, but Lyle's being detained."

"Why? What did he do?" she cried out.

"I think you should talk to Sheriff Tickman, ma'am."

Mrs. Sleeter glanced around the room. "Where is he? Where's the sheriff?"

Deputy Fitzgerald gently took her arm. "Come with me."

"Where are you taking me?" she demanded, yanking her arm away.

"Let's go talk somewhere a little more private."

Fitzgerald escorted her to an interview room and helped her into a chair. "Please, make yourself comfortable. I'll be back in a minute. Is there anything I can get you?" he inquired.

She looked up at him, despair written all over her face. "Please, tell me. What did he do?" she asked softly, tears in her eyes.

Deputy Fitzgerald hesitated, torn between wanting to help her and knowing he should remain quiet. It was not his place to inform her why her son was being held in a jail cell.

"You need to talk to Sheriff Tickman. I'll go get him." He started to leave the room, then turned around and looked at her. "Mrs. Sleeter?"

"Yes," she said.

"Lyle's in trouble. Big trouble. Due to the fact that he's a minor and you're his mother, you have the right to see him. When you do, I suggest you tell him not to answer any more of the sheriff's questions. And, it might be a good idea if you find him a good attorney."

2017

O_{ne}

$S_{aturday}$

"How does it feel, knowing that today is your last day on the job?" Deputy Laura Edwards asked Sheriff Tickman.

The sheriff looked up at her and smiled. "Weird. I've been on the job for forty-one years. Except for a few odd jobs when I was young, it's all I've ever done. I don't think I'm gonna like this retirement crap, Laura."

"Just think of all the things you'll be able to do now. Frances has been asking you for years to build a gazebo in your backyard. Now, you'll have the time to build it. No more excuses. You'll be able to visit your kids more. Plus, you can travel and see the world. You've done your job, Tic. And, you did it well. Now, it's time to enjoy life."

Sheriff Tickman frowned. "I'm not sure I'm ready. I'm already doing everything I want to do. It's Frances who wants to do all that other stuff. Not me."

Deputy Edwards smiled. "It's a done deal, Tic. No changing your mind now. Shaun is going to do a fine job. You've trained him well."

"Speaking of our new sheriff – where is he? I figured he would be here at the break of dawn, ready to take over."

"I'm not sure where he's at," Laura replied. "He'll probably be here in a few minutes. Are you done clearing your stuff out of his office yet?"

"Nah. I'll get it later. So, you're already calling it

his office. I get the feeling you can't wait for me to leave," the sheriff said, joking.

"You got that right. We're all sick and tired of having to look at your ugly face every day," she kidded.

"Who's on duty tonight?" Sheriff Tickman asked her.

"Bill. And, Joanne. She said she'd man the phones tonight if we save her some cake."

"So, I'm gonna have cake," Tickman stated. "It better be my favorite."

"It will be. Frances is taking care of the food. She guaranteed me that you'll be getting all your favorites."

Sheriff Tickman sat back in his chair and took in his surroundings. "I'm gonna miss this place, Laura," he said, with a catch in his throat.

Laura looked away. "You're going to make me cry," she said. "Let's change the subject."

Sheriff Tickman stood and looked around his office. "This room could use a coat of paint. Maybe, something a little brighter. You know, less depressing than this. . ." His voice broke, and he looked away. "I guess this is it."

Laura glanced over at him, tears welling up in her eyes. "Shit!" she exclaimed, as she started to cry. "Now look what you've done."

"I'm sorry," the sheriff exclaimed.

Laura stood up, grabbed her keys, and headed for the door. "I'll be back in a few minutes," she told him. As she exited the police station, she bumped into Cary's new sheriff, Shaun Fitzgerald.

"Hey, slow down," Sheriff Fitzgerald said.

"Sorry," Deputy Edwards muttered.

"What's the problem?

She smiled at him through her tears. "I'm just being a baby, is all. Nothing against you, Shaun, but I'm going to miss that big lug."

"We all are, Laura. They broke the mold when they made him."

"Thank God," Deputy Edwards said, grinning. "If they hadn't, we'd be living in a world of giants."

"Where are you going in such a rush?"

"I had to get out of there before I fell apart. I'm gonna go pick up some donuts."

"Make mine a sugar donut," Sheriff Fitzgerald told her.

"I know. I'll be back in a few."

Cary's new sheriff watched as she headed towards her car. She may be forty-six, he thought to himself, but that's sure one nice tight ass.

Sheriff Tickman glanced up as Fitzgerald walked into the police station. "Did you see Laura?"

Sheriff Fitzgerald shook his head yes. "She's just feeling a little blue. She went to get some donuts."

"She's not the only one feeling a little blue. Do you think I made a mistake, Shaun?"

"Well, seeing as how you retiring opened up the sheriff's job, I can't say you did." He grinned at the sheriff. "Seriously, Tic, you're gonna be missed a lot."

"For a few days, maybe. Then, before you know it, it will be like I was never here."

"I doubt that. Plus, we'll stay in touch," Fitzgerald said.

Mrs. Tickman and her youngest daughter had spent the afternoon decorating the banquet room. Sixteen tables were set, ready to accommodate the one hundred fifty guests that had been invited to her husband's retirement party.

The banquet room at The L & D Banquet Hall, in Crystal Lake, was packed and noisy, waiting for the guest of honor to arrive. Although the party wasn't a surprise, Mrs. Tickman had asked her husband to arrive a little after six. She determined that most of the guests would be there by six. By arriving a little late, he could greet the majority of his guests at the same time, rather one by one.

The bar was busy, most people taking advantage of the one-hour open bar before dinner. The bar would then close during dinner and re-open around nine o'clock.

Frances Tickman checked her watch for the third time in the past five minutes. It was now six-twenty and her husband hadn't showed. She decided to call him and tell him to get his butt in gear. She took out her phone and called him. No answer.

She glanced across the room and saw her daughter, Valerie, staring at her. Valerie shrugged, a questioning look on her face. Mrs. Tickman shook her head back and forth and mouthed "I don't know".

At seven o'clock, the head waiter asked Mrs. Tickman if they should serve the meal. Mrs. Tickman asked him if he could wait a few more minutes, as her husband, the guest of honor, had not yet arrived.

At seven-thirty, Mrs. Tickman told the head waiter to serve dinner to the guests before it was ruined. She mentioned to her daughter that she was going to drive home. "Perhaps, your dad had a flat tire or something," she said.

"He would have called you, Mom," Valerie told her. "I'm going with you."

"No. You stay here and make sure everything goes smoothly. I'll take our new sheriff with me," she told her daughter.

Sheriff Fitzgerald pulled into the Tickman's driveway and put the car into park.

"The lights are on in the kitchen," Frances Tickman commented. "Tic never leaves the lights on when he leaves the house."

"His car might be in the garage," the sheriff told her. "I'll check it out. You stay in the car."

"I'm coming with you," she stated, emphatically.

"Please, just stay here until I know everything is okay," Sheriff Fitzgerald requested.

Frances Tickman waited in the car while Fitzgerald looked through the garage window. He didn't give her any indication of what he had seen as he walked by his car and headed to the back of the house. He went up the back stairs that led to the kitchen, put his face to the window, and stared inside.

"Shit," he muttered softly.

"What!"

Fitzgerald jumped. "My god, you just scared the hell out of me." He turned and looked at Frances Tickman. "I asked you to stay in the car."

55

"What did you see?"

"Do you have a house key with you? I need to get in."

"Is Richard in there?"

"Frances, please, give me the key. Then, I want you to call 911 and get an ambulance here. Tic is lying on the floor. I can't see his face, but it looks like he's hurt."

"Oh, God. No!"

"Please, give me your key," he asked again, holding out his hand."

"Is he okay?" she asked.

"Now!" Fitzgerald said loudly. 'Or, I'm gonna break the damn window."

Frances Tickman reached into her purse and pulled out her keys. Her hand was trembling as she handed them to the sheriff.

"Now, please, call 911," Fitzgerald told her, as he unlocked the back door and entered the kitchen.

Two

Saturday and Sunday

"Don't come in here," Sheriff Fitzgerald yelled, as Frances Tickman took a step into the kitchen.

She stopped and stared at her husband. "No!" she screamed.

"Frances, please stay back. You can't be in here."

She stared at Fitzgerald, as if not understanding his words. "Richard?" she finally murmured, as the reality of what she was looking at sunk in. She locked eyes with Fitzgerald. "Please, tell me he's not dead."

"I'm so sorry, Frances." He walked over to her, put his arms around her, and held her as she broke down and started to sob. After a few moments, she put her hands on his chest and pushed away from him. She looked directly into his eyes. "You find the son of a bitch who did this, you hear?" she demanded, as she wiped the tears away with the back of her hand.

Fitzgerald looked away, trying to not get emotional.

"Shaun, promise me," she pleaded.

"I promise, Frances. I'll find him and, when I do, I'll make sure he pays for this," he told her.

"I want you to make the bastard suffer."

Cary's entire police force was crowded into the conference room. It had been almost twelve hours since Sheriff Tickman had been found. Most of the force had had little or no sleep, and emotions were running high.

The room went quiet as Fitzgerald walked into the room. He glanced around the table at his officers. Officer Sam Frankel immediately stood and offered his boss his chair. Fitzgerald waved him off, indicating he should stay seated.

Fitzgerald took a deep breath, trying to control his emotions before he spoke. "Okay, then. It looks like we're all here. Before we get into details, there's something I want to say. I worked with Tic for over twenty years. He pretty much taught me everything I know. He was a kind man and he was a fair man. He rarely lost his temper and I never saw him hit a prisoner. He was a loving husband and father. He wasn't one hundred percent sure if he made the right decision about retiring. We joked about it just yesterday; how his leaving opened the door for me to step into his shoes."

The deputy hesitated. He looked away. "Well, I'll tell you all right now, I wish I didn't have his job and I don't know if anyone could ever fill his shoes. I wish he was here, right now, guiding us, telling us what to do. The fact that my first case as sheriff is to find the person or persons who murdered him is killing me. What we need to do now. . ." His voice broke

"Sheriff?"

Fitzgerald looked over at Deputy Laura Edwards, who had interrupted him. "Yes."

"Can I get you something? Some water, perhaps?"

Fitzgerald smiled at her. "I've got some, Laura," he told her, looking down at the glass on the table in front of him. "Thanks anyway."

He looked around the room, taking in the faces of the men and women who were now his responsibility. He sighed. "Okay, I'll finish this up. The next few days are going to be rough. Mrs. Tickman is going to need all the support we can give her. Her family will be flying in for the funeral, so maybe she'll need someone to do airport duty and pick them up. Whatever. I want someone to coordinate everything for her and get it done. Anticipate her needs and take care of them. We need to help her get through this."

"I'll do it," Sally Thompson, the office clerk said.

"Good. Thank you," Fitzgerald replied.

"Now, let's go over what we know so far." He turned and looked at Deputy Edwards. "Laura, have you got the rundown for us?"

Laura shook her head yes and stood. "As we all know, when Tic didn't show up for the dinner last night, Frances got worried. Sheriff Fitzgerald drove her to her house to see if he was there. They were concerned he might have had car trouble or something had happened. They arrived at approximately 7:45 p.m. After the sheriff determined that Tic's car was in the garage, he walked to the back of the house. He looked through the back door window into the kitchen. It was then he saw a body lying on the floor. He also saw a massive amount of blood next to the body." She stopped for a minute and took a breath.

"You okay?" Sheriff Fitzgerald asked her.

"I'm fine." She hesitated a second. "All right, then," she continued. "He asked Frances to call 911, which she did. However, before Sheriff Fitzgerald could stop her, she stepped into the house and saw Tic's body. The sheriff escorted her out of the house, called the banquet hall, and informed Deputy Larson what had happened. The coroner was called and arrived at approximately nine o'clock. From that point on, forensics took over the crime scene. At approximately four o'clock this morning, Tic's body was removed from the crime scene and taken to the morgue by the coroner."

"Is it right that the word pervert was written in blood on the kitchen wall?" Officer Porter asked.

"It was. That's a fact that we'd like to keep under wraps for now. The less the press knows about this case, the better. Unfortunately, Frances saw the bloody message. By the time the paramedics arrived, she was not doing well."

"Which is totally understandable," Porter commented.

"Of course, it is. The paramedics did give her a sedative to calm her down, which seemed to help," Edwards continued. "She spent the night with a neighbor, where she and her daughter will be staying until the crime scene is released and the cleanup is done." Deputy Edwards glanced over at the sheriff. "That's pretty much it for now," she said.

"Our priority is to find this bastard," Sheriff Fitzgerald declared. "This wasn't a break-in gone bad and I don't think this was a coincidence. Nothing was taken from the house. Due to the severity of the beating, I'd say that this was personal. As we all know, Tic was a big man and in good shape. Whoever did this to him was strong, probably a lot younger, and most likely took him by surprise. There's a possibility that he wasn't working alone. Whatever the case, Tic was repeatedly hit with a heavy tool. The coroner thinks a hammer was probably the murder weapon."

The sheriff reached for his glass and took a sip of water. "There's a good possibility that someone was looking for revenge. Tic put a lot of people behind bars over the years. Check out the prisons and see who has been released recently who would have a grudge against Tic."

"That would be just about everyone," Officer Frankel commented.

"You may be right," The sheriff said, agreeing. "But we still need to check out the whereabouts of any persons who have been released from jail recently."

He took a deep breath and let it out. "Now, what I'm about to tell you is not to be repeated under any circumstances. I don't want this getting out to the papers either. Understand?"

The room was dead silent, his officers waiting for him to continue.

Fitzgerald closed his eyes and clenched his jaw, once again trying to keep control of his emotions. "His penis is missing. The son of a bitch, who did this, cut off his dick."

Three

Monday

"Can you guess who's back in town?" Deputy Laura Edwards remarked as she looked up from her computer.

Sheriff Fitzgerald continued concentrating on the file lying in front of him.

"Sheriff, I just asked you a question."

He looked over at her, giving her his full attention. "I'm sorry," he said. "What did you say?"

"Did you know that Lyle Sleeter is out of prison and has been living in Cary for the past three weeks?"

Sheriff Fitzgerald sat back in his chair and stared at her, a shocked look on his face. "You're not serious?"

"Totally. He was released three weeks ago. His conviction was thrown out."

"What the hell are you talking about? And, why wasn't our office notified?"

"Hold on." The deputy continued reading the information that was on her monitor.

Sheriff Fitzgerald watched her for a few moments. "Well!" he cried out impatiently. "What's the story?"

She held up her hand, indicating that he should wait for her answer. Finally, she shook her head in disbelief and stared at the sheriff. "The appeals court reviewed his case, determined there wasn't enough evidence for a retrial, and threw out the original conviction."

"Son of a bitch. I can't believe they let him out. I remember that case well. He was fifteen years old when he killed Marjorie Finnegan."

"I know. I was working here back then. I interviewed a lot of her neighbors."

"Although, now that I think about it, I really shouldn't be surprised," Fitzgerald told her. "We never really had any solid evidence and the kid swore he was innocent, but Tic was sure he had done it. The D.A. was good and managed to get Sleeter tried as an adult. The kid was convicted on circumstantial evidence. He was found guilty and sentenced to life in prison."

"What was it? Fifteen or sixteen years ago?"

"It was the summer of 2001, so that makes it sixteen years ago. Sleeter is thirty-one years old now." The sheriff stood and walked over to the front window. He was quiet, as he stared outside. "Do you think Tic was a good sheriff?" he asked Edwards.

She looked surprised. "Of course, I do. Why? Don't you think he was?"

He turned and smiled sadly. "Of course, I do. For the most part, anyway. However, when it came to the Finnegan case, he was dead set on blaming the Sleeter kid from the very beginning. Tic and I rarely had a difference of opinion, but we did when it came to that one."

"What are you saying? You didn't think the kid was guilty?" his deputy asked.

"Nope. I never did. I told him so from the very beginning, but he wouldn't listen."

"And, now Sleeter's out and you think he might have killed Tic. Is that it?"

"Just thinking out loud, is all. But you had to admit that Sleeter has a motive. Especially, if he was innocent. He might have decided to get even for having spent sixteen years in prison for a crime he didn't commit."

"I guess that puts him on top of our suspect list, doesn't it?"

"It just might. We better track him down and find out where he was Saturday night."

"I'd start with his parent's house. If he's back in town, that's probably where he's staying," Deputy Edwards declared.

"Who else do we have on that list?" Fitzgerald asked.

Deputy Edwards glanced over at him. "You really want to know?"

"Of course, I do."

"No one," she told him. "Right now, he's our only suspect."

"Have you checked how many prisoners have been released in the past year?"

"I not only checked it out but I went back five years. There were a ton of guys let out, but only a few from this area."

"How many were Tic's cases?" Fitzgerald asked.

"Six," the deputy answered.

"How many were recent releases?"

"One."

"Sleeter," he stated.

"That's right. Of the other five, two were released three years ago, one was released two years ago, and the other two were let out last year. None of them were violent offenders. I can't see any of them being angry enough to want to kill Tic."

"So, that leaves Sleeter."

"Right, but whoever killed Tic doesn't necessarily have to be someone that he put in jail. Who knows what else he had going on in his life, Shaun? I mean, we certainly don't know everything about each other, and everyone has their little dark secrets that they never talk about."

Sheriff Fitzgerald looked at her and smiled. "You mean you don't tell me everything? And, all this time I thought you were an open book."

"Kid all you want," she said, "but, right now, we have nothing to go on. We have one person who might have had a reason, but basically, we have zilch."

"That's just great."

"Are you gonna go talk to Sleeter?"

"I am, but I'm calling the D.A. first to find out what the hell happened," he told her.

"What about Tic's autopsy? Has Dr. Dempsey gotten back to you with her findings?"

"No. I expect to hear from her today. The crime scene guys did find a couple of prints. They were pretty smudged. I'm not sure if we'll get a hit on them. Other than that, we don't have anything."

"No footprints or tire marks or anything?" Deputy Edwards asked.

"Nada."

"Why do you think they cut off his penis?" Edwards asked. "It makes me sick just thinking about it."

"I haven't got a clue. Or, as far as that goes, why

write pervert on the wall? Tic was about as much a pervert as I am."

"There had to be a reason to write that, don't you think?"

"Not necessarily," Fitzgerald told her. "It could have been some nut job that killed him and it probably doesn't mean anything."

Edwards looked away. "Do you think we'll ever find it?" she uttered softly.

Fitzgerald stared at her. "Laura," he said in a firm voice, "you need to put that out of your mind. Understand?"

Edwards gave him a sad smile. "I'll try."

Sheriff Fitzgerald reached over to his phone and buzzed Sally, the office clerk.

"Yes?"

"Sally, will you get D.A. Bolton on the phone for me? If he's not in, leave a message asking him to call me back as soon as possible."

"I'm on it," she answered and broke off the connection.

F_{our}

M_{onday}

"Did you call first to see if the Sleeters are home?"

Sheriff Fitzgerald glanced over at his deputy and, then, looked back at the road in front of him. "Nope. I want to take them by surprise."

"Why?"

"So, they don't have time to get their stories straight," he replied.

"You're acting like the whole family was in on it," Deputy Edwards commented. "You haven't got a clue who might have killed Tic and you're fixating on Lyle Sleeter. Sounds a little like what you accused Tic of doing."

The sheriff bit his bottom lip, a sign that he was holding in his temper. "Right now, Sleeter is all we've got," he muttered after a few moments. "I'm just going to talk to him. That's all, Edwards."

"Sorry. I didn't mean it the way it came out. I know you wouldn't do that."

"Well, I didn't think Tic would do it either, but he did," Fitzgerald said. "So, maybe it was a fair statement after all." He smiled at her. "Keep me honest, Edwards. That's why you're here."

"So, that's the reason. Good to know," she replied, grinning. "There's the Sleeter house," she told him, as they turned onto Margaret Terrace. "It's the third house on the left."

Deputy Edwards fidgeted as she waited for someone to answer the door. After a few more moments she looked over at her boss and shrugged her shoulders. "It doesn't look like anyone's home," she commented.

"Cars are in the driveway. Ring the bell again."

"Maybe the bell's not working," Edwards muttered. She pulled open the screen door and knocked on the Sleeter's front door, then, stepped back as the door swung open, startling her.

"I wondered how long it would be before you showed up."

Edwards took another step backwards, lost her balance, and reached out to Sheriff Fitzgerald, who grabbed her arm. "Careful there, Deputy," he said. "We don't need to be making any trips to emergency today."

"Thanks," she replied.

Lyle Sleeter stood in the doorway, watching the exchange between the two cops, not saying anything.

Sheriff Fitzgerald looked up at him and grinned. "Good god, Lyle, what did they feed you in prison? Growth hormones? "

Lyle Sleeter was a big man. Sheriff Tickman had predicted Lyle might hit six feet two inches, but he was off by a good four inches. Sleeter was six feet six inches and weighed at least three hundred and fifty pounds. He smiled at the sheriff but didn't comment.

"I need to talk to you, Lyle."

"This is about Sheriff Tickman, isn't it?" Sleeter asked, figuring he already knew the answer.

"I'm afraid it is," Fitzgerald answered. "Is it all

right if we come in for a few minutes?"

"I'm not sure. This isn't my house. I guess I'll have to ask my mom." He turned, facing into the house. "Hey, mama," he yelled. "Is it okay for the sheriff and his deputy to come in?"

"Hell, no, it isn't," Lyle's mother shouted.

Lyle turned back to the sheriff, grinning. "You heard my mom. She said you can't come in."

"She's real funny, Lyle. Now, you tell your mom that we are either coming in to ask you a few questions or we'll have to escort you to our fine jail. Either way, we'll be asking. . ."

"Get your asses in here," Mrs. Sleeter interrupted, as she pushed her son aside, and smiled at Fitzgerald. "Kitchen," she ordered. "I've just put on a fresh pot of coffee."

"Sounds good," Sheriff Fitzgerald said, as he and his deputy entered the house and followed Mrs. Sleeter into her kitchen.

"You make one hell of a good cup of coffee," the sheriff said, as he put his cup down on the table.

"Thanks," Mrs. Sleeter replied, as she sat down across from him. "So, tell me, Sheriff. Just what are you here for?"

"I think you know," Sheriff Fitzgerald replied, as he looked at Lyle.

"I'll tell you right now, you cops aren't going to pin this one on my boy," Mrs. Sleeter said. "Lyle was home Saturday night. All night. In fact, he's been home every night since he got out of prison."

"Is that right, Lyle?" the sheriff asked.

Lyle grinned. "That's right, Sheriff. Just like my mama said. I was right here all night."

"Can anyone else verify that?"

"My dad was here," Lyle told him.

"Anyone else, besides family?"

Lyle looked over at his mom and smiled. "How many people were here, mama?"

Mrs. Sleeter, looking extremely smug, looked straight into Sheriff Fitzgerald's eyes. "We had a welcome home party for Lyle. There were probably twenty or twenty-five people here."

"I'm glad to hear that," the sheriff said. "Of course, I'll need to check it out, but it's just a formality at this point."

"Of course," Mrs. Sleeter replied. "I gather you want a list of the people that were here."

"I do."

Mrs. Sleeter looked over at Lyle. "Go get that list of names that are on the desk, would you?" she asked him.

"You've got a list prepared already?" the sheriff asked her, surprised.

"We knew you'd be asking," she answered, smiling.

"Well, then, I guess that's it for now." He looked over at Deputy Edwards, who was leaning against a kitchen wall, listening to the conversation. "Ready?" he asked her, as he stood up.

"Ready," she replied. As she started to leave the room, she turned and looked at Mrs. Sleeter. "What time?" she asked.

Mrs. Sleeter looked confused. "Time? What do

70

you mean, what time?"

"What time did your party start, Mrs. Sleeter?" Deputy Edwards inquired.

"Oh, the party. It started around seven-thirty. Why?"

"Just wondering, that's all," the deputy told her. She looked at Lyle. "And, you were here the entire day?"

"That's right," he said.

"You never left the house?"

"No, Deputy, I never left the house."

"Just to be clear, Lyle, you were here between six and seven-thirty Saturday night. Is that correct?"

"Yes," he replied.

"And, your party started at around seven-thirty?"

"That's right."

"So, the only people that can confirm that you were in the house between six and seven-thirty are your parents. Is that right?"

"What the hell, Deputy? I already told you that I never left the house all day."

Mrs. Sleeter glanced over at the sheriff; concern written on her face. "What is she getting at, Sheriff?"

"Sheriff Tickman was murdered sometime between six and seven o'clock. It seems that the only people that can confirm where Lyle was during that time are you and your husband."

F̲ive

M̲onday

"Do you think they're telling the truth?" Deputy Edwards asked as they pulled away from the Sleeter house.

"I think so. Laura, I doubt Lyle Sleeter has ever hurt anyone."

"He does seem like a pussy cat. Do you think he might be a little slow?" Edwards inquired.

"Lyle has an extremely high IQ. He was tested years ago. He was off the charts. I think it's just his personality. Plus, being in prison probably changed him. No, I think we're dealing with an extremely intelligent person."

"So, you think we can cross him off the list, then?" she asked.

"Not yet. Let's check out the party people. Plus, I want to check with his warden and find out what kind of a prisoner he was. You know, find out if he was a model prisoner or a trouble maker and how he related to the other inmates."

"We need to go back sixteen years and re-open the Finnegan case and start all over again, don't we?"

"We do. And, I think we should look at Michael Finnegan again," the sheriff replied.

"Do you know where he's living?"

"Same house. He's remarried and has a couple of kids.

"He owned a travel agency if I recall," Edwards commented.

"You recall right. He still does. Although, with the ease of booking your vacations online, I understand his business isn't doing well."

"I don't know how he can live in a house where his wife was murdered," Edwards said. "It seems a little creepy to me. I, sure as hell, couldn't do it."

"Different strokes and all that shit," Sheriff Fitzgerald said.

"I guess. When are you going to talk to him?"

"Later, after he gets home from work."

"So, where are we off to now?" Edwards asked him.

"I want to talk to Charlie Peters," the sheriff told her.

"He'll be delivering mail right now, won't he?"

"Nope. He's working inside now - sorting mail, waiting on customers, that kind of stuff. He's lucky he didn't lose his job for messing around with Marjorie Finnegan sixteen years ago. I guess his boss figured it was best to keep him off the street and away from temptation, so they put him behind a counter."

"His wife divorced him, you know," Edwards stated.

"You can't blame her," the sheriff said.

"Men are such pigs," Edwards said, under her breath.

Sheriff Fitzgerald looked at her, surprised. "Whoa!" he shouted. "Where did that come from? I'd say that Marjorie Finnegan was the pig in this case. She made the move on Peters, not the other way around. She seduced him, along with. . . Well, who knows how many men there were. We didn't scratch the bottom of the barrel, Laura, when we were investigating that case. I don't think it's fair of you to group all men into that category."

"He could have said no. All of them could have said no."

"Did you get a good look at Marjorie Finnegan? She was temptation personified." He grinned. "Hell, I would have probably hit it if I'd had the chance."

"And, you prove my point. All men are pigs."

"I take it back. She was married. I would never mess around with a married woman. That's just not a fair statement."

"Well, I'll take it back then."

"Thank you."

"Most men are pigs." She laughed. "Is that better?"

Fitzgerald grinned as he shook his head. "There's no winning with you, is there? I don't know why I even try."

"Me either," Edwards replied. "We're here."

"I know we're here. I'm driving. . ."

"Men drivers are the worst drivers," Edwards interrupted, grinning.

"Don't even start."

Sheriff Fitzgerald looked up as the door to the postmaster's office opened and a man walked in. The years hadn't been kind to Charlie Peters. He looked much older than his fifty-six years, and he walked with a limp. Besides being overweight, he had lost almost all of his hair and what was still hanging on was white.

Fitzgerald glanced over at Deputy Edwards, who mouthed "wow" as she looked back at him.

"You wanted to talk to me?" Peters asked.

"I do," Fitzgerald replied.

"I'm working. Can't we do this later?"

"We could, but I'd like to get this out of the way.

"Have a seat, Charlie," Postmaster Goodman said, motioning to a wooden chair next to a small conference table. She glanced over at Fitzgerald. "Do you need me for anything?" she asked.

Fitzgerald shook his head no. "We're good. This won't take long. Thanks, Mary."

"No problem. I'll be in the back. Let me know when you finish up," she told him.

Sheriff Fitzgerald waited until Goodman had closed the door, then, took a seat across from Peters. "I figure you've heard about Sheriff Tickman," he said.

"Of course. The whole town knows. But I don't see what that has to do with me."

"We're re-opening the Finnegan case. Lyle Sleeter is out of prison, and we are back to square one. We're interviewing everyone that was involved in that case again, and that includes you."

"Well, I sure don't know anything more than I did sixteen years ago. I saw her that day, got my rocks off, and I left. She was alive and happy when I last saw her and there's nothing new I can tell you. Anyway, we all know that Sleeter did it. Just because he got off on some dumb technicality doesn't mean he's not guilty. Can I go now?"

"No."

Charlie Peters gave him a dirty look and

75

slouched down in his chair. "Whatever."

"Sixteen years ago, were you aware that Marjorie Finnegan was making herself available to more men than just her husband and you?" the sheriff asked.

Peters looked away, thinking about his answer. After a few moments, he said, "I guess in a way I did. Back then, I didn't give it a lot of thought. It just happened between us. My god, Sheriff, she ran around that house half-dressed most of the time, wearing that skimpy little robe. It was there for the taking and I gotta admit that I took my share. There probably were a lot of others who had a piece of that sweet pie besides me."

"Do you know who else she might have been seeing besides Lyle Sleeter and Dan Samuels?"

"You mean that UPS driver? That surprised me when I heard about him. He didn't seem like her type."

"She had a type? What do you mean her type?"

Peters grinned. "Big. She liked big men. Samuels wasn't that big a guy. Her husband, Sleeter, me – we're all big guys. Of course, he could have had a big. . ." He glanced over at Deputy Edwards and smiled. "You get my drift."

Edwards gave him a blank stare.

"We get it," Fitzgerald told him. "You worked that route for years, Charlie. Think. Do you recall seeing anyone – men or women – going in and out of her house?"

Peters sat back in his chair and looked up at the ceiling. He pursed his lips and, then, he suddenly smiled. "I saw a cop car parked on the side of the house a few times," he declared.

"Get serious," Fitzgerald told him.

"I am. Sure, it was only a few times, and the squad was parked on the street, but I did see it. I don't know who was driving it, though. It could have been the sheriff." Peters grinned. "Hell, it could have been you for all I know. Were you bonking her, too, Sheriff?"

"Not funny, Peters." He glanced over at Edwards. "I think we're through here."

"Suit yourself," Peters said. "I guess you don't want to hear about the woman, then."

Edwards, who was taking notes, looked up. "What woman?" she asked.

"I doubt if this means anything and it was a long time ago, but I did see a woman at her house on a few occasions."

"Do you know who it was?" Sheriff Fitzgerald asked him.

"Nah., I seem to recall that she was a good-looking blond. I noticed her when I put the mail in Marg's mailbox on the front porch. The door was open, but I couldn't hear what they were talking about. Could have been the Avon lady for all I know."

"Could you identify her if you saw her again?" the sheriff asked.

Peters looked at the sheriff and laughed. "Ya, right. It was sixteen years ago, Sheriff, and I can barely remember what I did yesterday. What do you think?"

S_{ix}

M_{onday}

"Who was that?" Jenny Finnegan asked her husband, as he ended a call and laid his phone on the kitchen table.

"Sheriff Fitzgerald. He's on his way over."

"Why?" Jenny asked, looking concerned.

"He didn't say, but I figure it has something to do with Sleeter being released from prison."

"Why would you know anything about that?" she inquired. She hesitated for a moment, then, asked, "Should I put on a fresh pot of coffee?"

"You know I don't drink coffee this late," Finnegan replied.

"I meant for the sheriff."

"Hell, no. What do you think we are – a restaurant? If he wants coffee, he can buy his own damn coffee," he said, raising his voice.

Jenny Finnegan studied her husband's face, wondering why he was so upset. "Just asking, is all," she commented.

Michael Finnegan gave her a dirty look, pushed his chair away from the table, and stood up. "Get that table cleaned up," he ordered, as he walked out of the kitchen and headed toward the living room.

"House could use some paint," Officer Sam Frankel muttered under his breath.

"It is starting to look a little run down," the sheriff said, agreeing with his officer. "I understand his business isn't doing too well. Maybe, he's having a hard time."

Just as Sheriff Fitzgerald was about to ring the doorbell, the front door swung open. Michael Finnegan was standing there with a big grin on his face and a drink in his left hand. "Long time no see," he said loudly. "How they hanging, boys?"

"Michael," the sheriff said, acknowledging him. "Thanks for seeing us on such short notice."

"No problemo," Finnegan replied. "Come on in. Can I get you something to drink?"

"No thanks," Fitzgerald and Frankel said in unison.

"Well, I'm going to have another one," Finnegan said. "Take a seat. I'll be with you in a moment."

Sheriff Fitzgerald watched while Finnegan walked into the kitchen.

"I think he's drunk," Officer Frankel said quietly.

"Maybe. Maybe not. I'll bet you anything that he's putting on a show."

"Why would he do that?" Frankel asked.

"So, if he says anything that might be incriminating, he can say he didn't know what he was talking. . ." Sheriff Fitzgerald stopped talking, as Finnegan came back into the living room, carrying a fresh drink.

"Sure, I can't get you one?" Finnegan asked as he plopped down in a chair.

"We're good, thanks," the sheriff replied.

"What's this about, anyway?" Finnegan asked as he took a large sip of his drink. "Ahh. That's some smooth shit," he declared.

The sheriff stared at Finnegan, not responding. He watched while Finnegan took another sip of his drink, and then burped loudly.

"Whoops. Sorry about that," Finnegan said, laughing.

Sheriff Fitzgerald stood up and stared at Finnegan, obviously disgusted with the man's actions. "Forget this. You're drunk."

"Am not," Finnegan responded.

"Well, if you're not, you sure are acting like you are. Obviously, there's no point in trying to talk to you tonight."

"I'm not drunk. Ask me anything you want." Finnegan said, grinning.

"I don't have time to play your games. I want you in my office tomorrow morning – eight o'clock sharp."

Finnegan shook his head no. "That's not good for me, sheriff. I have a business to run, you know." He sat back in his chair and sighed. "I'm not drunk. Just ask your damn questions and get out of here, will you?"

"Are you here alone, Michael?" the sheriff asked him.

"My wife's in the kitchen. I have no idea where my boys are. Why? What do you want them for?"

Sheriff Fitzgerald turned to Officer Frankel. "Sam, will you please ask Mrs. Finnegan to come in here?"

"What do you need her for?" Finnegan yelled as Frankel headed to the kitchen.

"I'm right here, Sheriff," Jenny Finnegan said, entering the room. "What do you want?"

80

"I want to see your husband in my office at eight o'clock sharp tomorrow morning. Can you see to it that he makes it on time?"

"I'll try. . ."

"She's not my damn babysitter," Finnegan yelled.

"Michael, please," Jenny begged.

"Just get back in the kitchen," Finnegan yelled at her. He looked up at Sheriff Fitzgerald. "There's no reason to bring my wife into this," he said loudly.

"I want you to understand that you need to show up, Michael. Understand?"

"All right. I'll be there, but I still don't know why we can't do this now."

"It's simple. I need you to have your wits about you when I talk to you. It's obvious that you're in no condition to have any type of discussion right now."

"He's not drunk," Jenny shouted. "It's all a big act so he won't have to talk to you. Isn't that right, Michael? Tell the sheriff that you're just a big fake."

"You shut the fuck up," Michael yelled.

"Or, what?" Jenny shouted back. "You gonna hit me again? Come on, big man. Let's see you get all tough in front of the sheriff."

Michael jumped up off the chair and took two threatening steps toward his wife. As she backed away, Officer Frankel grabbed his arm and pulled him away. He looked at Sheriff Fitzgerald questioningly.

"Cuff him," Fitzgerald told Frankel. He looked over at Jenny and saw the scared look on her face. He suddenly realized how much courage it had taken for her to stand up to her husband.

"You know what, Mrs. Finnegan? I do believe that your husband is drunk and a threat to you right now. I think it might be a good idea if we took him down to the station and let him sleep it off there."

"The hell you are," Michael Finnegan yelled. "She's right. I'm not drunk. Test me. You'll see."

"We'll sort this out down at the station." He watched as Officer Frankel put the cuffs on Finnegan.

"I'll sue your ass, Fitzgerald," Michael Finnegan yelled, as Officer Frankel escorted him out the front door.

"This only makes things worse," Jenny Finnegan told the sheriff.

"If he so much as touches you again – ever - I want you to call me immediately." He looked at her. "Jenny? Do you understand? Look at me."

She glanced over at him and shook her head yes. "I understand," she whispered.

"How long has he been like this?"

Jenny looked as if she was going to start crying. She took a deep breath and tried to get her emotions under control. "It's just that everything is going to shit. His business is failing, the boys have been acting up in school, and we aren't getting along – obviously. He's just under a lot of stress and I seem. . ."

"You're getting the brunt of it. Right?" the sheriff asked her.

"I guess. He's a good person, Sheriff Fitzgerald. It's just all this. . . I don't know what to do."

"Jenny, there's no excuse for a man to hit a woman – ever! Do you want to file charges against him?"

"God, no. It's not like he beats me or anything. He's just slapped me a couple of times."

"That's a couple of times too many. I'll talk to him and keep him in jail tonight. It'll give him some time to think about it."

"Please, don't. Besides, what would I tell the boys? Just let him go, will you? God, I shouldn't have said anything," she said, starting to cry.

"It's gonna be okay, Jenny. I'll take him down to the station and talk to him. Okay? I'll warn him about hitting you and the trouble he'll be in if he hurts you again. That's all."

"You'll let him come home, then?" she asked.

"I will. But only if he behaves himself. If he tries anything or gets stupid, he'll spend the night as my guest in jail. Deal?

Jenny looked up at him and gave him a little smile. "I guess. Thanks, Sheriff."

"How long have you and Jenny been married?" Sheriff Fitzgerald asked Michael Finnegan.

Finnegan stared at the back of the sheriff's head. "This is ridiculous, you know. I'm not drunk and you have no right to arrest me. I didn't do anything wrong."

"You were going to hit your wife."

"No, I wasn't. Do you think I'm stupid enough to hit her in front of a couple of cops?"

Fitzgerald glanced in his rearview mirror and looked at Finnegan, who was sitting in the back of his squad. "Actually, I do. So, how long?"

"What difference does it make?"

"Just curious, that's all."

"We've been married for fifteen years."

Sheriff Fitzgerald was quiet for a moment. "You didn't waste any time after Marjorie was killed, did you?"

"You know, she looks familiar," Officer Frankel commented.

"Who does?" Fitzgerald asked.

"Mrs. Finnegan. What was her name before you married her, Michael?"

The sheriff looked over at Frankel, wondering what he was getting at.

"She was Jenny Blatter, wasn't she?" Officer Frankel asked Finnegan.

"So, what if she was? What's that got to do with anything?" Finnegan replied.

"Well, if I remember correctly, she was your secretary sixteen years ago."

"Ya. So?"

"So, she was also your alibi when your wife was murdered."

Seven

Monday

Sheriff Fitzgerald pulled into his parking space in front of the police station and turned off the ignition. "Let's go," he said, as he got out of the car.

Officer Frankel exited the squad, opened the back door so Finnegan could get out, and escorted him into the station. "Room One?" he asked, as he glanced over at the sheriff.

"That's fine. I'll be there in a minute. You want a cup of coffee, Michael?"

"No, I don't want any fucking coffee," Finnegan replied.

"Can the attitude or you'll be spending the night here. I told you before; I just have a few questions to ask you. I don't know why you're making this so hard on yourself."

Finnegan sighed. "Whatever. Let's just get this over with."

Thirty minutes later, Sheriff Fitzgerald walked into Interview Room One and sat down at a table across from Michael.

"About damn time," Michael said, sarcastically.

"Where were you Saturday night between six and seven-thirty?" the sheriff asked, ignoring Finnegan's attitude.

"What?" Finnegan asked, looking confused.

"Where were you Saturday night between six and seven-thirty?"

Finnegan sat back in his chair and stared at the sheriff. "You're serious?"

"Dead serious."

"Between six and seven-thirty? Hell, I don't. . . Wait. I was at Harry's baseball game."

"Who's Harry?" the sheriff asked him.

"My son. He plays baseball. They had a game Saturday night."

"And, you were there the whole time?"

"Of course, I was. Ask my wife or any of the other parents that were there."

"I intend to."

"Do you know that Lyle Sleeter is out of prison?"

"I do. I was notified that he was being released."

"How do you feel about that?"

"How do you think I feel? I'm mad as hell. There's no way he should be free after what he did."

"You mean killing Marjorie?"

"What else would I mean?"

"Well, she was having an affair with him."

Finnegan sneered. "That wasn't an affair. She didn't have affairs. She just used those men for sex. She never reached a climax, and she was horny all the time. Always hoping she'd get off the next time. According to the doctors, she was what they call a nymphomaniac. It was great for me, though." He leaned back and looked up at the ceiling. "I guess I should have done more to help her."

"Did you know about the other men, Michael?"

Finnegan thought about the question for a few moments. "I suspected something was going on, but I never faced up to it. Didn't want to rock the boat, you know." He was quiet for a few seconds. "Now that I think about it, I guess I probably knew she was messing around. I did hear rumors about it. Hell, I even heard that Sheriff Tickman stopped by a few times. I don't know if it's true or not. I sure as hell hope not."

"Who did you hear that from?" Sheriff Fitzgerald asked.

"I can't remember now. It was a long time ago."

"Try to remember, Michael. It's important."

Finnegan shrugged. "I don't remember. What difference does it make now? It was sixteen years ago and Marg and Tickman are both dead. Who cares?"

"I do. I care. If Sleeter didn't murder your wife, then who did? I've got an unsolved case here, Michael."

"Well, don't look at me. I sure as hell didn't kill Marjorie and you know it."

"Right now, I don't know jack shit. I have to re-open a sixteen-year-old case and it pisses me off."

"That's not my problem," Finnegan commented.

"How long have you been beating your wife?" Sheriff Fitzgerald asked abruptly, changing the subject.

Finnegan started to stand up, caught himself, and plopped back down in his chair.

"I don't beat my wife," he said, angrily. "I've never hit her. Jenny can be a little bitch and we aren't getting along right now. She just said that to piss me off."

"Well, it looks like she succeeded," Fitzgerald said. "You have a temper, Michael. I've seen you get angry more than once tonight."

"You just accused me of hitting my wife. That would make anyone angry."

"She told me you've hit her a few times."

"Lies," Finnegan commented. "She's looking for sympathy, that's all."

"So, if I let you go back home, are you gonna slap her around?"

Finnegan gave a big sigh and stared at the sheriff. "I've never hurt her. We fight sometimes, but it's never physical. Ask the boys if you don't believe me. They'll tell you that I've never hit her. I don't know what else I can tell you."

"I'm going to check out what you said about being at your son's game Saturday night."

Finnegan grinned. "Be my guest."

"Don't leave town, either," Sheriff Fitzgerald added.

"I'm not going anywhere. Don't worry."

"Were you having an affair with Jenny while you were still married to Marjorie?" the sheriff asked, wanting to see if he'd get another angry reaction from Finnegan.

Michael smiled, surprising the sheriff. "She was my secretary. That's all."

"If I ask her that same question, what will she say?"

"That she was my secretary. . ."

"You don't want to lie to a cop, Michael."

"All right. We messed around a few times, but it wasn't serious."

"Did Marjorie know about it?"

Finnegan didn't answer.

"Well?" the sheriff asked.

"I don't honestly know. I never told her and it never came up. I don't think so."

"Okay, then. I guess that's about it. I'll have Officer Frankel give you a lift home. But, first, I want you to write down the names of the people that can confirm that you were at your son's baseball game Saturday night."

"Answer me one question, Sheriff," Finnegan said.

"What's that?"

"Why in the world do you think I would kill Sheriff Tickman? I hardly knew the man. I don't understand your thinking at all."

"You don't have to. And, maybe it's not Tickman I think you killed. Maybe, you're back on my list of suspects for Marjorie's murder."

"What the fuck," Finnegan yelled. "You know I didn't kill her."

"Do I? Just write down the names of the people who can confirm where you were Saturday."

Eight

Tuesday

"Dan Samuels is living in a retirement village in Huntley." Deputy Edwards looked up from her computer and glanced over at her boss. "Did you hear me?"

"I heard you," Sheriff Fitzgerald replied. "Sun City?"

"Right."

"He seems kinda young to be living in a retirement place. Is he over fifty-five?"

Edwards checked her monitor. "No, but his wife is. She's seven years older than him. Are you going to go talk to him?"

"Is he still working for UPS?"

"No. He's on disability."

"So, he should be home," the sheriff said.

"I'd call first if I were you. Just because you're retired doesn't mean you sit home all day. He could be out."

"Give him a call, will you? Set up something for today." He grabbed the keys for his squad off his desk and headed towards the door.

"Where you going," Edwards asked.

"Did you know that Sarah Montgomery is alive and is still living across the street from the Finnegans?"

"No friggin' way," the deputy exclaimed. "She must be a hundred. . ." She thought for a moment. "She's ninety-three years old."

"I don't know about that, but she's still kicking. I'm gonna go talk to her."

"Can I go with you? Please, pretty please."

"Why?" the sheriff asked, puzzled by his deputy's excitement.

"I interviewed her after Marg Finnegan was killed. She was one cool old lady back then. I've just got to see what she's like today."

"Laura, you've got a ton of work to do here. I want you to start checking that list that Finnegan gave us last night."

"You mean the people that saw him at his son's baseball game?"

"Exactly. Get on that, will you?"

"As soon as we get back from Sarah Montgomery's house," she said, grinning. She reached for her hat. "Let's go."

Sarah Montgomery didn't look a day older than she had sixteen years ago. She might have gained a few pounds and shrunk an inch or two, but other than that, she looked great. She opened the door with a big smile on her face. "Officer Edwards," she stated. "It's been a long time since you've come to visit."

"It's Deputy Edwards now," Laura told her. "And, you're right. It has been a long time."

"And, who is this handsome young man you brought with you?"

"Sarah, this is my boss, Sheriff Fitzgerald."

"Ah, that's right. The old sheriff was murdered. What a shame. He seemed like such a nice man. It's nice to meet you, Sheriff."

"Ma'am," the sheriff replied. "It's a pleasure to meet you. Deputy Edwards has told me a bunch of nice things about you."

"Well, isn't that sweet of her?" She watched as the sheriff made a strange face. "Something wrong?" she asked.

"I'm just trying to figure out what that smell is."

Sarah laughed. "I'm pretty sure you know what it is and it's legal. I have the start of glaucoma and I have a prescription from my doctor. Sorry, Sheriff, but you won't be arresting me today."

Sheriff Fitzgerald grinned. "I wouldn't dream of putting a lady like you behind bars."

"Would you like a cup of tea?"

"Yes, please," Deputy Edwards said before the words were barely out of Sarah's mouth. "I'd love a cup." She turned and looked at her boss. "Sheriff, you have to try her tea. It's wonderful."

"Why thank you, dear," Sarah said, as she glanced over at the sheriff. "Would you like to try my tea?" she asked him.

"I guess I could go for a cup. Thanks," he told her.

"Sit. I'll be back in a minute," Sarah said, as she hurried into the kitchen.

After Sarah had served her guests their tea, she sighed and sat down in an overstuffed chair. "So, you must be here for a reason."

"We are," Edwards replied. "By the way, is Emma McDonald still living in the neighborhood?"

Sarah shook her head no. "No. She died a few

years ago."

"I'm sorry to hear that. I know you two were close," Edwards said.

"We were, but she got real fucking funny a few years back. Her son had to put her in a home."

The sheriff's head jerked up and he looked over at his deputy, who was grinning.

"Well, you certainly look great and, obviously, you're as sharp as a tack. Anyway, Sarah, have you heard that Lyle Sleeter is out of prison?"

"I heard that," Sarah replied. "And, good! I never did think that poor boy killed that woman."

"Maybe, not. But that means we're going to re-open the case and we were just wondering if you remember anything else that might help us?" Sheriff Fitzgerald asked.

Sarah looked confused. "What do you mean? I told you police everything I knew back then."

"Yes, Sarah, but sometimes memories will creep into our minds years after something happened. Have you ever recalled something that didn't seem important at the time?" he asked.

Sarah Montgomery slowly picked up her cup of tea and took a sip. She set it back on its saucer and looked the sheriff in the eyes. "I don't think it's anything you'd want to hear."

"And, why would that be?" Deputy Edwards asked her.

"It wouldn't make any difference now, anyway," Sarah said, softly.

"It might," Edwards said. "What is it?"

"Well," Sarah started, "We think that Marjorie

Finnegan had a few more visitors than what we talked about sixteen years ago."

"Who do you mean by we?" the sheriff asked.

"Me and Emma and a bunch of other people who lived in the neighborhood back then. We had a little get-together after the Sleeter boy went to prison and the murder came up during our conversation. We started putting together a list of people that we saw go in and out of that house while Marjorie was still alive."

"Really?" Sheriff Fitzgerald commented. "So, you figure we didn't get a complete list?"

"I know you didn't," she replied emphatically.

"Who did we miss?" Fitzgerald asked.

"Like, I said. It doesn't make any difference anymore." She glanced over at Deputy Edwards and smiled. "More tea, dear?"

"Yes, please," Edwards said and held out her cup for a refill.

"Sheriff?" Sarah asked.

"I'm good. What's your secret?"

"My secret?"

"I'm not a tea drinker. To tell you the truth, I don't care for tea. But this is the best cup of tea I've ever had. What's the secret ingredient?"

Sarah Montgomery beamed at the compliment. "Why, thank you. It's exactly what you said. A secret."

"Okay, I get it," the sheriff said, grinning. "You won't tell us that, but how about telling us who else was on that list."

Sarah was quiet for a few moments, thinking about her answer. "Sixteen years ago, we had milkmen who delivered milk right to our front doors. Do you

94

remember that?" She looked at the two police officers, waiting for a response.

"I kind of remember," Edwards said.

"I do," the sheriff replied.

"Good. The milkman delivered milk to the Finnegan's twice a week; on Wednesdays and Saturdays. Not many people got it back then. Milk delivery, I mean. A long time ago, almost everyone had their milk delivered. It was nice, but things changed. Anyway, once in a while, his truck would be parked up the street from the Finnegans' in the afternoon. We didn't think much about it back then, but later, when we talked about it, we were pretty sure he was visiting Marjorie Finnegan. It was never parked there very long and none of us ever saw him go in the house, but. . . Well, you put two and two together and you get four."

"Do you remember his name?" Sheriff Fitzgerald asked.

"Of course, I do. We put it on the list."

"And, it was?"

"Albert – Albert Gregory. He's dead, though, so don't go looking for him."

"I remember him," Edwards said. "He owned Gregory's Dairy. It closed back in. . ." She thought for a moment. "Back in 2004. Albert had a heart attack and died. He was quite young if I recall. They closed the dairy right after that."

"You're close, dear," Sarah said. "Only it was 2005, not 2004."

"Oh. Sorry."

"That's all right. You can't be expected to remember everything," Sarah told her, smiling.

"Who else is on that list," Sheriff Fitzgerald asked.

"Well, I hate to tell you, but we added Sheriff Tickman," Sarah said, looking down. "He was on the list. But, he's dead now, too." She looked up and smiled. "Besides the ones you knew about, that's all the names we put on the list. There were more men that visited her, but we didn't know who they were. There were a few women that visited her, too, but we never found out who they were."

"Tickman?" the sheriff muttered. "You think he was playing around with Marjorie?"

"We figure he was. If it wasn't him, it was one of you cops. A squad car used to be parked on the side of her house once in a while. Well, not exactly on the side of the house. It was always up the street a way. As I said, we put together a list of men we thought she might be fucking and he was on it."

Deputy Edwards started to laugh.

"Get it together, deputy," the sheriff said, glancing over at her. "So, it's just gossip," he stated. "No one actually saw him with her."

"Well, what do you think he was doing there?" Sarah asked him.

Fitzgerald stared at her for a moment, then, looked away. "I haven't got a clue." He glanced at Edwards. "I guess we should be going."

"Tell me, Sheriff, do you think that Sheriff Tickman's death has anything to do with Marjorie's murder?" Sarah asked as he stood to leave.

"Why would you ask that?"

"Just a feeling, that's all."

Sheriff Fitzgerald slammed his car door shut and glanced over at Deputy Edwards.

"What?" she asked him.

He put the key in the ignition and started his squad car. He looked over at her again, a questioning look on his face.

"What?" Edwards said again. "Do I have something on my teeth?"

"What the hell does she put in that tea? I feel ten years younger."

Deputy Edwards grinned. "She does make one hell of a cup of tea, doesn't she?"

Nine

Tuesday

Dan Samuels was at home, living out his few remaining days hooked up to numerous tubes that were keeping him alive and pain-free until his heart finally said enough. Mrs. Samuels escorted the sheriff into a large, cheery bedroom and yelled, "Hey, asshole, the law wants to talk to you."

Sheriff Fitzgerald looked over at her. "I didn't realize that your husband was ill," he told her. "Is this a bad time?"

She grinned. "Any time is a bad time, but if you have anything to ask Dan you better do it now. There's no guarantee he'll be here tomorrow."

"I can hear you, bitch." Dan Samuels said, his voice so low it was almost a whisper.

"Up yours," Mrs. Samuels retorted, as she turned and walked out of the room.

Fitzgerald glanced at Deputy Larson, who shrugged and shook his head.

"Mr. Samuels," the sheriff said loudly, "I'm Sheriff Fitzgerald and this is Deputy Larson. Are you strong enough to answer a few questions?"

"I'm not deaf. You don't have to yell," Samuels replied, in a low husky voice.

"Sorry. I thought. . ."

"You thought because that bitch of a wife of mine yelled, I was hard of hearing. Well, I'm not. She just likes to yell at me. She's been yelling at me for sixteen years now. I should have divorced her back

98

then, you know. After Marg was murdered and the shit hit the fan. Well, I didn't and I've been paying for it ever since." He sighed deeply, reached over, and pushed a small button.

Sheriff Fitzgerald looked at him questioningly.

"Morphine."

"Cancer?" the sheriff asked.

"Yep. And, I'm about to hit that button one more time, so if you have anything to ask me, you best do it fast."

"Actually, Dan, I've had to reopen the Finnegan case. I suppose you heard that Lyle Sleeter is out of prison and back home."

"I saw it on the TV. The bitch doesn't tell me anything. If it wasn't for TV, I wouldn't know what's going on." He grimaced, obviously in pain. "Could you hurry this up, Sheriff?"

"I just wondered if there was anything you might recall about Marjorie's death that you might have overlooked back then," the sheriff said. "Perhaps, since then, you've remembered something that might be important."

Dan Samuels turned his head and looked out the window.

"Dan?" the sheriff said, after a few moments, thinking that perhaps Samuels had drifted off.

"She was so gorgeous, you know. Do you remember? It hurt when I found out about the other men, but I guess a woman like her. . ." His voice trailed off and he stopped talking.

"I'm sorry to bring this backup. I realize this is difficult for you."

"There's nothing," Samuels said, softly.

"I'm sorry," Sheriff Fitzgerald said. "I didn't catch that."

Dan Samuels looked at the sheriff. "I don't have anything to add. I can't help you." He reached for the button and pushed it. "Nighty night."

"Is he dead yet?"

Sheriff Fitzgerald and his deputy turned to see Mrs. Samuels standing in the doorway.

"Do you really hate him that much?" Deputy Larson asked her.

She stared at Larson for a moment, then, turned away as her eyes watered up. "He was my everything, you know. I guess you could say he still is. So, the answer is no, Deputy." She glanced over at the bed, then back at Larson. "I love him. Always have."

"But, then, why. . ."

"We need to get going," the sheriff interrupted, as he turned to leave the room. "Let's go, Deputy."

"I don't get it," Deputy Larson declared, breaking the silence.

Sheriff Fitzgerald glanced over at him, and then back at the road. "What don't you get?"

"If she loves him, why treat him like that?"

"Love takes many forms, Larry. I'm not about to try to figure it out. But I figure she's never gotten over him cheating on her."

"Then why stay with him? Why not just get a divorce and get on with your life?"

"Hell, I don't know. She loves him? Can't leave him? Can't forgive him? Wants to punish him? It's a mystery to me."

Deputy Larson sighed. "I guess. Women are weird, aren't they?"

Sheriff Fitzgerald laughed. "You better keep that thought to yourself, Larry."

"You're really pursuing this Finnegan thing. It's been sixteen years. Why not just let it go? It seems to me that you should be spending your time trying to find out who murdered Tic."

Sheriff Fitzgerald stared at him for a moment before looking back at the highway. He stopped his squad car at a red light and looked over at his deputy again. "It seems to you? Are you saying you don't think I'm doing my job, Deputy?"

Deputy Larson's face turned red. "God no. I'm sorry. That came out all wrong. I just meant. . . I just wondered. . ." He looked away. "I didn't mean it the way it sounded, Sheriff. I'm sorry."

"All right. Forget it."

The light turned green, the sheriff turned his squad left and headed toward the police station. "I'm working both cases, Deputy. I'm not slacking off trying to find Tic's killer, but. . ."

"I know and I'm sorry," Larson interrupted.

"Don't interrupt me when I'm talking," Fitzgerald said, starting to get angry.

"Sorry."

The sheriff took a deep breath and let it out. He pulled into the parking lot in front of the station and turned and looked at Larson. "I'm pretty sure that the two murders are somehow connected."

"What? Are you serious?"

"I know it sounds crazy, but I just have this gut feeling that Tic found out something about Finnegan's murder and was killed before he could say anything. I'm trying to put the pieces together."

"That's a reach, Sheriff," Deputy Larson said.

"You think I don't know that? But whatever it is, I want to go slow this time. No jumping to conclusions or making mistakes."

"You mean like Tic did?" Larson asked.

"What do you mean, like Tic did?"

"Hell, Sheriff, everyone in town knows that Tic railroaded that Sleeter boy. Nobody thought he was guilty except for Tic and the D.A. It seemed like they wanted to close that case as fast as they could and Sleeter was the fall guy."

As Sheriff Fitzgerald reached for the door handle, he turned back and looked at his deputy. "I'd keep those kinds of thoughts to yourself, Larry. Tic was really loved here in town – kind of a hero to a lot of people. Talking like that could make a lot of people mad."

"I guess," Deputy Larson replied. "But there are also a lot of people in this town that are still upset over Lyle Sleeter being in prison for sixteen years for a murder he didn't commit."

Ten

Tuesday and Wednesday

"Do you have that rundown for me?"

Deputy Edwards looked up from her computer and glanced over at her boss. "I've got a few more people to talk to, but I figure they'll just tell me the same thing that everyone else has."

"Which is?" Sheriff Fitzgerald asked.

"That Lyle Sleeter never left the party the night Tic was killed. We have his mother and father, who will swear that he never left the house for the entire day, and about twenty-five guests who will testify that he was home all night."

"Okay, so he was home all night. But, it's the six to seven-thirty thing that bothers me. His mother and father are his alibi and you know, as well as I do, that parents will lie to protect their kids."

Deputy Edwards smiled. "He's anything but a kid, Sheriff."

"You know what I mean."

"Anyway," Edwards commented, "I've got a few people who can confirm that Lyle was home the entire day."

Sheriff Fitzgerald looked surprised. "Who would that be?"

Deputy Edwards glanced down at the paper on her desk. "Joanne and David Beal, Roger and Patricia Siddell, and Captain Jack."

"Captain Jack?" Fitzgerald asked smiling. "Who the hell is Captain Jack?"

Edwards grinned. "Jack Starling. He was a Captain in the Army and his friends still call him Captain. The Beals, the Siddells, and Captain Jack all confirmed that Lyle Sleeter was working in the yard most of the afternoon and was definitely outside and at home between six and seven-thirty."

Fitzgerald was quiet for a few moments.

"Well?" Edwards inquired.

"Take Sleeter off the list of possible suspects. If he's got that many people willing to testify that he was at home during the time Tic was murdered. . ." He hesitated. "Well, that's good enough for me."

"Will do. What about the few people I haven't interviewed yet?"

"Forget it," Fitzgerald told her.

"You know what this means, don't you?" Edwards asked him.

"What time is it?"

Edwards checked her watch. "Quitting time. At least it is for me. My shift is over. Why? What are you thinking?"

"You want to go get a drink?"

"Where?"

"Does it make a difference?" the sheriff asked her.

"I've got a brand-new bottle of Jim Beam just begging to be opened. How does my place sound?"

Fitzgerald grinned. "Sounds good. You got anything there to eat?"

"How about we order a pizza?" Edwards replied.

Fitzgerald nodded his head yes. "Works for me. I'll meet you at your place in about fifteen. I've got a phone call to make."

Deputy Edwards stood up and walked towards the front door. She glanced back at the sheriff. "Shaun?" she said.

"What?"

"You know what this means, don't you?" she asked again.

"Of course, I do. It means that I'm out of suspects and that we haven't got a fucking clue about who murdered Tic.

"Just coffee is fine," Deputy Edwards told Frances Tickman. She watched as the woman poured her a cup of coffee and set the pot back on the warmer. "Thanks, I need this. I'm not quite awake, yet."

"Rough night?" Frances asked.

"I'd say it was more late than rough," Edwards said grinning.

Frances gave her a slight smile and sat down in a chair opposite Edwards.

"How are you holding up, Frances?" Edwards asked. "Is there anything I can do for you?"

Frances looked up at her and shook her head no. "Not really. The funeral parlor has taken care of most of the arrangements. The kids will all be here later today. I guess the only thing left for me to do is to pick up Richard's dress uniform from the cleaners and take it over to the. . ." She looked away, trying to control her emotions. "I'm sorry," she said, tears running down her cheeks.

"Don't be. I know how hard this is. Why don't I

do that for you?"

"Oh, would you? That would be so nice of you."

"I'll do that as soon as I leave here." Deputy Edwards took a sip of her coffee. "That sounded strange just then, when you said Richard. It's been so long since I've heard anyone call him that, I had almost forgotten his first name," she said.

"Laura, I wonder if you'd do something for me."

"Of course. Anything you want, just ask."

"Do you trust Shaun?"

Laura looked surprised at the question and glanced over at Frances. "Why would you ask me that? Of course, I do. I've worked with him for years. I'd trust him with my life."

Frances stood up and walked over to the sink. She looked out a window that overlooked the backyard and sighed.

"Frances, what is it?" the deputy asked.

"I found something while I was going through some of Richard's stuff. I'd like you to take a look at it and tell me what you think. But you mustn't tell anyone, especially not Shaun."

"What is it?" Laura asked.

"Promise you won't tell anyone?" Frances said.

"Of course, but why not Shaun? Perhaps, he could help."

"No!" Frances exclaimed. "I don't want him involved." As she turned to look at Laura, her hand hit her coffee cup that was on the counter, knocking it into the sink. "Shit."

"Did it break?"

"Forget it," Frances said, loudly. "Just forget I

said anything.

"Please, Frances, tell me what it is. I won't say anything to Shaun. I promise."

Frances Tickman looked her in the eyes for a moment, then, looked away. "It's nothing. Really," she said. "Thanks for coming over, Laura. I appreciate it."

Laura studied her for a moment, then, stood up. "You know if you need anything, all you have to do is ask. I mean it, Frances. Anything at all."

Frances smiled. "Of course, I do. And, you'll still pick up the cleaning for me?"

"Of course," Laura said. "Well, I guess I better get going. Call me if you need anything else."

Frances Tickman watched as Deputy Edwards opened the back door. "Bye, Laura," she called out softly.

"Bye," Edwards responded. "See you later."

"Laura?"

"Yes," she answered, turning back to look at Frances.

"Please, be careful."

Eleven

Wednesday

"You're late. Where have you been?" Deputy Larson asked as Edwards walked into the Cary Police Station.

"Running an errand for Frances Tickman. Is the boss in?"

"He's in the john. I think he's under the weather. He looks like hell." Larson looked at Edwards as she plopped down at her desk. "So do you," he added.

"Do what?"

"Look like hell. Are you sick, too? Stay away from me if you are."

"I'm not sick," Edwards replied, testily. "I'm just tired."

"Late date, huh?" Larson asked, grinning.

Edwards started to answer him, changed her mind, and reached into her desk drawer. "Shit!" she exclaimed.

"What?" Sheriff Fitzgerald inquired, as he pushed the door to the bathroom open and walked into the room. "What are you shitting about?"

"My bottle of aspirin is gone. Someone stole my aspirin. This is a police station for crying out loud and someone working here is a thief."

"No one stole your aspirin," Fitzgerald said quietly. "The bottle is on my desk."

"Oh," Edwards said. "I'm sorry I yelled." She looked at Fitzgerald and motioned for him to come closer.

"What?" he inquired, not moving.

"Can I talk to you for a minute – alone? Your office?" she asked softly.

"Can it wait?" Fitzgerald asked her.

"It could, but it shouldn't."

"What does that mean?" He closed his eyes for a second and sighed. "Christ, I've got such a headache. What the. . ."

"Your office, please," Edwards said, practically whispering.

"Fine. Let's go."

Deputy Edwards followed the sheriff into his office and shut the door. She grabbed the bottle of aspirin and opened it, removed two, and swallowed them.

"How can you do that without water?" Fitzgerald asked her.

"I had coffee with Frances this morning," she said, ignoring his question. "She called and woke me up a little after six."

"No wonder you're so crabby. You didn't get much sleep last night, did you?" He grinned.

"What's so fucking funny?" she asked.

"I guess I better tuck you in earlier next time. You certainly aren't a morning person, are you?"

"And, just what makes you think there's gonna be a next time?"

"Oh, there's going to be a next time."

Deputy Edwards stared at him, trying to think of a smart-ass response. She broke eye contact and looked away.

"So, what did you want to talk to me about?" the

Sheriff asked her, getting serious.

"As I said, I had coffee with Frances this morning. She had something. . ."

"How is she doing, by the way?" the sheriff interrupted.

"Fine. She's doing fine."

"Is everything set for tomorrow?"

"Yes, everything is set. Will you let me finish, please?" Edwards said, raising her voice.

"Christ, you're in a mood. Sorry. Please, go on."

"She wants me to – rather, she wanted me to do her a favor. And, she didn't want you to know about it."

Fitzgerald looked surprised. "She said that? That she didn't want me to know about it?"

"Ya. When she asked me to promise I wouldn't tell you what she wanted me to do, I hesitated. And, that was that."

"You have no idea what the favor was?" Fitzgerald asked, concerned.

"Nope. She said she found something in Tic's stuff, but she didn't say what it was. I imagine that, whatever it was, it concerned you. I mean – like, why else would she want to keep it a secret from you?"

"That's jumping to conclusions," Fitzgerald said. "You don't know that for sure."

"You're right. I don't. Anyway, she changed her mind and dropped it. Do you have any idea what she was referring to?"

"Nah." He sat back in his chair and was quiet for a few moments, thinking. "Nope. I can't think of one thing."

"It's gonna be a real circus tomorrow, don't you think?" Edwards asked. "I figure half the town will show up for Tic's funeral."

"You're positive she didn't want me to know about it?" Fitzgerald asked.

"I'm positive. Look, Shaun, it probably isn't anything. She's grieving and confused right now, trying to figure out why Tic was murdered. She probably found something and is making more out of it than it is. Just forget it."

"I just don't get it, that's all," Fitzgerald murmured. "I should go talk to her and find out what it's all about."

"No! Don't do that," Edwards said, abruptly. "Don't stir up the pot. Drop it! Please." She stood up and started pacing back and forth. "Shit. I never should have said anything."

"Why are you so upset? If there's something that could lead us to who killed Tic, I should know about it."

"I'm sorry I mentioned it. How about we just get through tomorrow and get Tic buried? I'll try to get a chance to talk to Frances alone and see if I can find out anything more. Just give me a couple of days and if nothing comes of it, then you talk to her. What do you say?"

"I guess that would be okay." Sheriff Fitzgerald sat back in his chair and gave Edwards a little smile. "Deal," he said after a few moments. "You feeling any better?"

"A little. The aspirin is starting to kick in. How about you?"

"Ya, I'm feeling better, too. I just need a good night's sleep."

"Me, too." Edwards smiled. "Last night was fun, wasn't it?"

"The best time I've had in quite a while, even if I do feel like a Mack truck has run over me."

"That's the booze. We drank way too much last night."

Fitzgerald laughed. "You think? We almost finished that bottle. Next time, let's cool it."

"Oh, you still figure there's gonna be a next time, do you?" Edwards asked.

"I thought that question was already answered," the sheriff said, as he reached for the bottle of aspirin.

"Ya, you feel better all right," Edwards kidded.

Twelve

Thursday

Deputy Edwards had been right when she predicted that half the town would show up for Sheriff Tickman's funeral. St. Peter's Catholic Church had been filled to capacity and the overflow of people stood outside on the church steps and the sidewalk in front of the place of worship. A couple of loudspeakers had been mounted on the front of the building so that the service could be heard outside of the church.

After the funeral service concluded, the mourners drove to the cemetery where a traditional gravesite military funeral was held, which included three rifle volleys, the playing of taps, and the presentation of the American flag to Mrs. Tickman.

Following the graveside service, the majority of mourners gathered in the church basement for a pot luck meal that had been prepared by the Ladies Guild. Approximately one-half of the people present managed to be served the meal before the food ran out. Mrs. Tickman's son, John, apologized to the people standing in line waiting to eat and asked them to please leave the church.

After the members of the Police Department had fulfilled their duties at the funeral, they assembled back at the police station. Sheriff Fitzgerald thanked them for their outstanding service and asked them to bow their heads and he said a prayer in honor of Sheriff Tickman.

"There were a lot of pissed-off people," Deputy Edwards said, as she sat down at her desk. She looked at her watch to check the time. "It's been a couple of hours since we sent those people home. I figure a lot of them headed to the bars instead of going home. I wouldn't be surprised if we have quite a few problems tonight."

Deputy Larson stuck a piece of gum in his mouth and started to chew. "I figure you might be right," he mumbled.

Edwards reached over and picked up the phone. "What's up, Sally?" she asked the receptionist. She listened for a moment, then, hung up the phone.

"Where's the sheriff?" she asked Larson.

"I'm not sure. He went out somewhere."

"Get hold of him," she instructed Deputy Larson. "Tell him to meet me at the Tickman house."

"What happened," Larson inquired.

"It seems that someone broke into their house during the funeral. The place has been tossed."

"Noo!" Larson moaned. "What the fuck is wrong with people?"

"Just get in touch with Shaun, will you? Bill, you're with me," she told Officer Porter. "Let's go."

John Tickman met Deputy Edwards and Officer Porter at the front door. "Thanks for getting here so fast," he said. "The place is a mess, so be careful where you walk."

"Where's your mom?" Edwards asked him.

"Everyone's in the kitchen. It seems to be the only room that wasn't practically destroyed."

"Have you guys touched anything?" the deputy asked, as she followed John into the kitchen.

"Only in the kitchen. Mom made good and sure we didn't touch anything in any of the other rooms."

"Good. Smart lady, your mom."

John smiled. "You learn a little being married to a cop for all those years."

"So, you don't know if anything is missing?" Porter asked.

"Not yet. Like I said, we looked but we didn't touch."

Deputy Edwards stood at the kitchen door and took in the room. Frances Tickman and her family were gathered around the kitchen table. Frances stood up when she saw the cops and walked over to them. Edwards held out her arms to hug Frances and Frances stepped into them, trying to hold back the tears.

"I'm so sorry, Frances," Edwards said. "I'll do my best to find out who did this."

Frances backed away and looked at Edwards. "I know you will, Laura. God, how can. . ." Her voice broke, as she started sobbing.

Deputy Edwards held her, patting her back. "Shh. It will be okay," she said softly.

"I'm sorry. I don't know why I'm crying. I'm more angry than anything. Sons of bitches that did this should rot in jail," she said loudly. "What kind of low life breaks into your house while you're burying a loved one?"

"The scum of the earth," Porter answered. "It's our fault, too. We should have had someone here watching your house. This kind of stuff happens all the time and none of us thought about having a house sitter here."

"It's nobody's fault," Edwards said. "It doesn't do any good to start looking for someone to blame. Let's get started, Officer Porter. We're going to treat this as a major crime. Get forensics out here ASAP. We're going over every inch of this house and if there's one fingerprint – hell, even if there's a part of a fingerprint – that this s.o.b left, we're gonna find it. Got it?"

"Got it," Officer Porter replied and looked over at the back door as it swung open.

"Deputy," Sheriff Fitzgerald said, as he stepped into the kitchen and acknowledged Edwards. He glanced over at Frances and nodded. "Frances, I'm so sorry for all of this."

"Sheriff Fitzgerald," Frances Tickman said formally. "No need for you to be here. Laura is doing a fine job."

"Hey, I'm sure she is. But, another pair of eyes never hurts. Right?" He glanced over at Deputy Edwards, a questioning look on his face. "What have you got so far, Deputy?"

"We're just starting in. Porter just called forensics and they should be on their way. I told Frances that we're gonna go over every inch of her house."

"Good. That's good," Fitzgerald commented. He looked over at Frances. "Is anything missing?"

"I have no idea. We haven't gone through anything, yet."

"Well, what we usually find is that the thieves

get in and out as fast as possible. They usually go for computers, electronics, jewelry, that kind of stuff. What about jewelry or money, Frances? Do you keep any valuables in the house?"

"Not really. Richard and I keep . . ." She hesitated a moment. "I store my important papers in a fireproof safe, but I don't keep a lot of money in the house. The only jewelry I have of any value are my wedding rings, and I never take them off."

"Where do you keep your safe?" Fitzgerald asked.

Frances smiled. "Richard was a smart guy, you know. He hid it in plain sight, so to speak."

"And, just where would that be?" Edwards asked.

"The end table next to the couch. The one by the window. Pick it up, and the safe is under it. Tic hollowed the table out. He figured that no one would lift an end table if they were robbing our house. It seems kind of silly now, seeing as how we didn't have anything worth very much to put inside of it."

"Larson, go see if that table's been disturbed," Sheriff Fitzgerald said. "Look - don't touch."

Larson was back in a few seconds, smiling. "Doesn't look like it's been disturbed to me," he told Fitzgerald. "The lamp and a figurine are still on it. I figure if they moved the table that stuff would be on the floor."

"Frances, I'd still like you to check out the contents to see if anything is missing. After it's checked for prints, of course."

"I'll do that, Sheriff. But I think I'll do that after

everyone has left the house."

Fitzgerald looked surprised. "It would help to know if anything is missing," he told her.

"If I find that anything of any importance has been taken, I'll let you know. However, Officer Porter already indicated that the table wasn't disturbed, so I don't think we have anything to worry about. Besides, like I said, there's nothing valuable in it. I doubt anyone was looking for our insurance papers, or wills, and stuff. I don't think there's anything to be concerned about, Sheriff."

"Just let me know if anything is missing," Fitzgerald told her.

"Of course, if any of our pictures were missing, I'd really be upset," Frances said.

"Not to worry, mom," John Tickman said, who was listening to their conversation. "Last time I was here, dad told me he saved all your pictures to the computer and backed them up onto a flash drive."

"I know, dear," Frances told him. She looked at Fitzgerald. "But I found a few pictures recently that he didn't back up. It would be a shame if those were missing."

By seven o'clock that evening, forensics had finished going through the Tickman home and had left. Although they found numerous fingerprints, they now had to determine which ones belonged to the Tickman's family, friends, and neighbors. Any unknown prints would be run through the FBI fingerprint recognition system and, hopefully, a suspect would be found.

Frances Tickman stood in her doorway, watching the last squad car drive away. She turned to her family, who were sitting in the living room, and said, "All right, guys. Let's get this mess cleaned up."

Her youngest daughter, Valerie, sighed and slouched back in her chair. "Can't it wait until tomorrow, Mom? I'm beat."

Frances sat down next to her daughter and put her arm around her. "We're all beat, sweetie, and, yes, it can wait until tomorrow. How about we call the Holiday Inn and get some rooms?"

John smiled. "That's a great idea, Mom. Let's do that."

"But, not you."

"What do you mean, not me?" John asked, confused by his mom's statement.

"I think someone should stay here tonight. Would you mind?"

"You don't really think that whoever did this is coming back?"

"I doubt it, John, but you just never know. However, I'm not about to take that chance. You know where your dad's gun is?"

"Same place?"

"Same place," Frances said. "Get it after we leave and, if anyone tries to break in, shoot the son of a bitch."

Thirteen

Thursday

Deputy Edwards pulled her squad car into her assigned parking spot in front of the police station and turned off the ignition. She reached into her breast pocket and took out a folded sheet of paper. She turned on the overhead light in the car, opened the paper, and read the note.

"Shit!" she exclaimed. She looked out of the car window and sighed. "Shit," she said again, softly. She read the note one more time, then, tore it up into little pieces, dropped them out of the window, and watched as the wind blew them into the street.

"That's littering, you know."

Edwards jumped at the sound. She turned to see Officer Porter standing by the side of her squad car. "Christ, Bill, you scared the crap out of me. What are you doing there, anyway?"

"I saw you pull in and was waiting for you to get out of your car. I thought you might like to go get a drink."

"Hold on a minute." Edwards put the window up and exited her squad car. She smiled at Porter, who was waiting for her to shut the car door.

"Well? What do you say? Are you up for a drink or two?" he asked again.

"Thanks, but not tonight," Laura said. "I'm pooped. It's been a long day and I had a rough night last night. What I need right now is a good night's sleep."

"I thought maybe you'd like to talk," Porter told her.

Edwards gave him a questioning look. "About what?" she asked him.

"About the note that Frances Tickman handed you before we left her house. And, the fact that she treated the sheriff like he was poison. What's going on, Laura?"

"Nothing is going on," Edwards retorted. "She just wants to talk to me, that's all."

"And, she doesn't want Fitzgerald to know about it, right?"

Edwards looked away, not responding.

"You'll feel better if you talk about it, you know," Porter told her.

"There's nothing to talk about."

"Then, why are you so upset?"

"Seriously, Bill, I'm not upset. I really don't know what Frances wants to talk to me about. All I know is that, whatever it is, she doesn't want Shaun to know about it. And, I don't want to get in the middle of whatever is going on. If there actually is anything going on."

"You don't have any idea at all what this is about?" Officer Porter inquired.

"None. But it must have something to do with Shaun. I mean, like, why else is she trying to keep this from him?"

"Well, whatever it is, she sure as hell is pissed at him about it. When does she want to talk to you?"

"Tomorrow. She wants me to call her and set up a time to meet."

"Are you gonna call her?" Officer Porter asked.

Edwards sighed. "Maybe. I don't know. I'm too tired to think about it and my bed is calling me."

"You should call her first," Porter suggested. "It might be something to do with Tic's murder."

"You know that Shaun thinks Tic's murder may be connected with the Finnegan case, don't you?"

"I heard something like that," Porter replied. "What do you think?"

Laura smiled. "Nothing. My brain has shut down and I'm done thinking." She started to walk towards her car, then, turned back towards Porter. "Let's keep this between us, okay?"

"Don't worry," he said. "My lips are sealed."

"What?" Deputy Edwards yelled as she answered her cell phone. She glanced at the time. It was exactly two-thirty.

"Laura? Are you awake?"

"Shaun? What's up?"

"Get over to the Tickman house. There's been a shooting."

"Who?" Laura held her breathe, as she waited for an answer.

"John Tickman."

"God, no. What happened?"

"I don't know. I just got the call. I'm on my way over there now. Meet me there."

Deputy Edwards pulled up in front of the Tickman house and glanced around. The ambulance was in the driveway, and the sheriff's car was parked on the lawn in front of the house. She heard sirens as she started to get out of her squad car, and waited until Deputy Larson pulled up alongside of her before she got out of her vehicle. She glanced over at Larson, frowning. "What the hell are you blaring those sirens for? You woke up the whole neighborhood."

Larson, ignoring her question, started running towards the house.

"Larry," Edwards yelled.

Larson stopped and looked at her. "What?"

"Slow down. The sheriff's in there. He's got everything under control."

Deputy Larson looked at her for a moment, letting her words sink in. "Right," he said. "You coming?"

"I'm right behind you," Edwards said. "Do you know what happened?"

"Nah. Just that Tic's son was shot. Do you know how bad it is?"

"Nope. That's all I know, too."

Deputy Larson walked into the living room a few steps ahead of Edwards. "Sheriff," he said. "What's going on?"

Edwards moved to Larson's side and glanced over at the couch, where John Tickman was sitting, looking perfectly okay. "John, are you okay?" she asked.

"I'm fine," he replied. "And, I'm a hell of a lot better than that dead son of a bitch in the kitchen."

She looked questioningly at Fitzgerald. "Sheriff?"

"Sorry. The call I got said John was shot, not that he did the shooting."

"Well, thank God he's all right. Who's in the kitchen? Where's the rest of the family?"

"I don't know who it is. He didn't have any identification on him. We're running prints. Frances and her family went to the Holiday Inn for the night. John stayed here and was sleeping on the couch when he heard a noise in the kitchen. He rolled off the couch and crawled behind that chair over there and waited. The intruder entered the living room and headed right for the end table. John stood up, yelled 'don't move', and the guy started running towards the kitchen. John fired and the guy made it as far as the kitchen before he went down."

"Was he dead when you got here?" Larson asked the sheriff.

"The paramedics called it a couple of minutes before you arrived."

"Did he say anything?"

"Nothing," Fitzgerald replied.

"So, everyone but you decided to stay at the Holiday Inn," Edwards said to John. "How come you didn't go?"

"After what happened today, Mom thought it would be a good idea if someone stayed here tonight."

"Where did you get the gun?" Edwards inquired.

"It was dad's. I wasn't going to sit here and not be able to defend myself if some asshole decided to try robbing us again," John said.

Edwards looked over at the sheriff. "Was the intruder carrying?"

"He was. He had a .45 on him when we got here. As far as I'm concerned, John acted properly. He was defending himself and his mom's property." He glanced at John. "We will need to take your statement later today, though, John."

"I know. No problem."

"Was there anyone else who knew your family would be staying at the motel tonight and figured the house would be empty?" Deputy Larson asked John.

"That's the strange part. It was a last-minute decision to stay at a motel. We didn't decide that until after you cops had left. It was mom's idea. So, the answer is no. No one else knew."

"And, you said the intruded walked right over to the end table?" Edwards inquired.

"Yep. He walked right to it. No hesitation."

Edwards looked at Sheriff Fitzgerald. "No one knew where the safe was hidden until Frances told us this afternoon. Doesn't this all seem a little fishy to you, Sheriff?"

"Let's not jump to conclusions, Deputy."

"I'm not. It's just that. . . Well, before today, no one, except family, knew where that safe was. So, how the hell did that dead guy in the kitchen find out?"

Fourteen

Friday

"Dan Samuels died last night." Sheriff Fitzgerald declared as he walked into the police station, carrying a box of donuts.

"Ya, I know. I heard it on the news this morning. It's really a blessing. He was in a lot of pain when we talked to him on Tuesday," Deputy Larson said. "They mentioned his involvement in the Finnegan murder. I don't know why they had to bring that shit up. It was years ago, for god's sake."

"Well, you know the media. Always looking for a big story," the sheriff said.

"I guess. It just seems that they always make more out of everything than they need to," Larson commented. "Did they say anything about when the funeral is going to take place?"

"No. At least, I didn't hear anything about it."

"Have you found out who it is that John Tickman shot last night?" Deputy Larson asked, changing the subject.

"Ya. The guy's name is Jerry Fritz. He was an ex-con who used to live in Crystal Lake. He was in prison a couple of times. I heard he was a real badass."

"What was he in for?"

"Served three years for breaking and entering in 2001 and had an assault charge in 2011. He beat the crap out of a guy in a bar fight. Almost killed him. He got five years for that. I didn't find anything else after that."

"So, where's the connection to the Tickmans or was it just a random break-in?" the deputy asked.

"It wasn't random," the sheriff replied. "His prints matched the partial we found after the first break-in. Obviously, he didn't find what he was looking for the first time and decided to try again. The problem, though, was that he didn't think anyone would be in the house. Big mistake."

Deputy Larson was quiet for a moment. "You said his name was Fritz, right?"

"Ya. Jerry Fritz. Why?" the sheriff asked.

"The name is familiar. Did we ever arrest him?"

"I didn't find anything in our records." The sheriff stared at Larson. "You know something?"

"I know that name. Let me think about it. It will come to me," he replied.

"You need a refill?" the sheriff asked, as he reached for the coffee pot.

"I'm good," Larson replied, as he stood up and headed for the front door. "I'm heading over to the high school. I'm giving a talk this morning about the horrors of using your cell phone while driving."

"You mean the dangers, don't you?"

"Nope."

"You're taking the slides," the sheriff stated.

"Oh, ya. I'm gonna show those kids' body parts lying all over the highway and try to scare the crap out of them. Did you know that one of the slides shows a detached arm and the hand is still holding a cell phone?"

"Jeez, Larson. Don't you think that's going a bit

too far?"

"Scare them today and maybe they'll put those damn phones away," Larson said, as he walked out, grinning.

The Holiday Day Inn, just outside of Crystal Lake, is known for its buffet breakfast. Deputy Edwards watched Frances Tickman as she scooped a spoonful of scrambled eggs onto her plate, wishing she would get her ass back to the table. Edwards didn't want to be here with Frances. She was regretting having called her and setting up this meeting. She didn't want to hear the woman's big secret or whatever it was. She wanted to run out to her car and drive away, never knowing the big news that Frances was about to tell her.

"The food here is great," Frances said, as she set her plate on the table and sat down. "Are you sure you don't want anything to eat?"

"Coffee is fine, thanks. I've never been a big breakfast person."

"Well, it's the most important meal of the day. My mother used to tell me. . . "

"Frances, I'm sorry to interrupt but I've got to get to work. Do you suppose you could tell me what I'm doing here?"

Frances shoved a forkful of eggs into her mouth and looked over at Deputy Edwards. "Sorry, she said and finished chewing. "Laura, I have information that would rock this town if it got out. I'm not sure what to do with it."

"I don't know what you're referring to, Frances.

But whatever it is, I think you should be having this discussion with Sheriff Fitzgerald."

"That's the problem. It involves Shaun and I can't talk to him. In fact, it involves both Shaun and Richard and I. . ." She looked away, trying to control the tears that were starting to fill her eyes. She reached into her purse and pulled out a tissue. "I'm sorry. I'm just so upset over this."

"Perhaps, it would be better if we talked later. You know, when you're not so upset."

"No!" Frances said loudly. "You need to know this and you need to keep it from Shaun. Don't you get it?"

"No. I don't," Edwards said, emphatically. "I have no idea what you're talking about."

"I have pictures of Shaun with that Finnegan woman," Frances blurted out.

Edwards' head jerked up and she stared at Frances. "Marjorie Finnegan?"

"Yes," Frances replied.

"What kind of pictures?" she slowly asked.

"What kind do you think?" Frances said.

"I see. How explicit are they?"

"As explicit as you can get," Frances replied.

"You said on the phone that this involves Tic. What's his connection?"

Frances started crying again and indicated that Edwards should wait a moment. She dabbed her eyes, blew her nose, and took a deep breath. "There are also pictures of my son of a bitch husband with his johnson hanging out. I have pictures of a number of men in all kinds of compromising positions while enjoying the late Marjorie Finnegan."

Edwards sat back in the booth, looking shocked. "Are you saying that both Shaun and Tic were messing around with that woman?"

"I don't know how she did it, Laura. I had trouble. . ." She looked away, trying to keep her emotions under control. "Never mind. Actually, I have pictures of her with almost a dozen different men."

"Who are they? The other ones, I mean."

Frances gave a short nasty laugh. "Mostly the ones we knew about. I'm not familiar with some of the men in the pictures. Do you know what's funny? There's no picture of her with Lyle Sleeter. Doesn't it seem strange that there's no picture of the person who was convicted of her murder?"

Deputy Edwards was quiet, while she thought about what Frances Tickman had just told her. "You think Shaun hired Jerry Fritz to break into your house to get those pictures, don't you?"

Frances looked at Edwards, not answering.

"He knew Tic had them hidden somewhere in your house and he wanted to get them before you found them," she said, thinking out loud. She looked at Frances. "I'm right, aren't I?"

"It makes sense to me," Frances said.

"But you must have gone into the safe from time to time," Edwards said. "Why didn't you find them before now?"

"The pictures weren't hidden in the safe. They weren't even in the house."

"Do you have them with you?" Edwards asked her.

"No."

"Where are they?"

"In a safe place, that only I know about."

Deputy Edwards was quiet, wondering what her next step should be. "What are you going to do, Frances?" she finally asked.

"I'm not sure. If these pictures come out, Richard is going to be a suspect in Marjorie Finnegan's murder. I'll be opening a can of worms."

"So would Shaun and some of the other men in those pictures be suspects, Frances. Anyone of them could have killed her."

"I know. I just don't want to drag Richard's name through the mud. This is exactly what will happen if these pictures get out.

"Even if Shaun was behind your house being robbed, we still don't know who killed Tic or why," Edwards declared.

"Well, we know Sleeter didn't kill him," Frances said.

"We're pretty sure. No, we're positive. He does seem to have a solid alibi," Edwards stated.

"Some of the men in those pictures have died. I'd be ruining a lot of families if the killer is dead and those pictures got out. And, that includes my family and it would all be for nothing. There'd be no arrest or trial, and it would destroy. . ." Frances sighed. "You get the picture, Laura. I just don't know how to handle this."

"Shaun thinks that the two cases are connected, you know."

"I've heard that," Frances responded. "I don't

take much of what he says at face value, right now. But, what do you think?"

"I'm beginning to think he's right. Especially now, with what you've told me. It's just that I can't put my finger on the connection. Even if Shaun and Tic were messing around with Marjorie, why was Tic murdered sixteen years later? Is there any connection between Lyle Sleeter being released from prison a few weeks ago and Tic's murder? And, where did Tic get those pictures that you found?" Edwards took a deep breath. "I'm sorry, but there are too many questions, Frances. And, I'm afraid I can't answer any of them."

"Here's one more. How do you think that Fritz guy knew where the safe was?"

"What do you mean?"

"John said he walked right toward it. He knew exactly where it was. That means that someone who was in my house yesterday had to have told him. And, I'm pretty sure it wasn't any of my family or one of the paramedics."

"God, Frances. You're pointing a finger at a cop. That's pretty hard to swallow."

"Let me ask you something else. Laura."

"What's that?" Edwards replied.

"Are you sleeping with Sheriff Fitzgerald?"

Deputy Edwards stared at Frances Tickman, her face turning bright red. "What the hell business is that of yours?" she asked, starting to get angry.

"Are you?"

"You know, Frances, I don't need this crap. I knew coming here this morning was a mistake."

"I need to know whose side you're on, that's all."

"If you're suggesting that I'm going to tell Shaun about this conversation, you're wrong. You know you can trust me, Frances."

"Can I? You didn't deny having an affair with him," Frances stated.

Edwards looked away. "We're not having an affair," she said softly.

Frances sat back and studied Edwards. "But you've slept with him, haven't you, Laura?" she said, after a few moments.

"It was just one time. Believe me, it won't happen again."

"I need to know I can trust you, Laura."

Deputy Edwards looked straight into Frances Tickman's eyes. "You can trust me, Frances," she said.

Fifteen

Friday

"You're late. Again." Officer Porter declared as Deputy Edwards walked into the police station.

"Is the sheriff here?" Edwards asked.

"No, he's out on a call. Why? What's going on?"

Edwards stopped in front of Porter's desk and looked at him.

"What?" Porter asked, starting to feel uncomfortable.

"How would you like to have that drink tonight?" she asked him.

"Seriously? I'd love to," Porter answered, grinning.

"Don't get all excited, Bill. There's something I need to talk to you about, that's all. How about we meet at Bushman's Inn around six?"

"What's it about?" Porter asked.

"Later," she whispered, as the door opened and Sheriff Fitzgerald walked in.

"Morning," the sheriff said.

"Good morning," Edwards answered. "Have you talked to Jerry Fritz's parents yet?"

"I've barely had time, Deputy. Why?"

"I thought I'd drive over and talk to them if you hadn't already. You know, maybe find out if they know what he was up to after he got out of prison."

"Fine. Take Frankel with you."

"He's out, Sheriff," Porter told him. "I could go with her."

Sheriff Fitzgerald hesitated for a moment. "No. I need you here right now. Are you okay going on your own, Laura?"

"No problem. I'll see you in a bit," she said. She picked up the keys to the squad car and headed towards the door.

"Did she seem like she was in a hurry to get out of here?" Fitzgerald asked Porter.

Officer Porter shrugged. "Didn't notice," he replied, as he looked down at his keyboard and started typing.

Deputy Edwards pulled her squad car into the driveway and turned off the ignition. She sat back and stared at the house. "Wow!" she exclaimed to herself as she exited her vehicle. She checked out the landscaping while she walked to the front door and rang the bell. "Some big bucks here," she muttered, waiting for someone to answer the door.

The deputy was about to ring the bell again when the door swung open. "May I help you?" an attractive woman asked. The woman noticed the police car parked in the driveway and took a closer look at Edwards. "You're a cop. Is there a problem?"

"Mrs. Fritz?" Edwards asked.

"Yes?"

"I'm sorry to bother you, ma'am. I'm Deputy Laura Edwards of the Cary Police Department. I'm so sorry for your loss."

"Thank you. Is that all?" Mrs. Fritz asked, starting to shut the door.

"No, ma'am. I wonder if I could have a few

135

moments of your time? I'd like to ask you a few questions about your son"

Mrs. Fritz, looking annoyed, hesitated. "No." She started to close the door, then, changed her mind. "I don't mean to be rude," she added, "but I don't have anything to say. Jerry quit being my son a long time ago. I haven't seen or spoken to him in years, so there's nothing I can help you with. Now, if you'll excuse me, I'm busy."

Deputy Edwards, taken back by the woman's cold attitude, turned and looked at the woman's yard. "You have a beautiful place here," she said. "Your landscaping is absolutely breathtaking."

Mrs. Fritz smiled at the compliment. "Why thank you," she responded. "We take a lot of pride in our yard."

Edwards started to leave, then, turned back and smiled at the woman. "I don't mean to bother you, but just one more thing. I was wondering if you know where your son was living. We don't seem to be able to find an address for him."

Mrs. Fritz was quiet for a moment, then, swung the door open. "I guess it would be okay if you come in for a couple of minutes? Would you like a glass of iced tea?"

Edwards smiled again. "Why, that would be lovely. Thank you so much," she said and followed Mrs. Fritz into her home.

Two hours later, Deputy Edwards was back at the police station, talking on the phone with the manager of the Crystal Lake Bank. His mother may not have seen or spoken to him since he had been released from prison in 2004, but she definitely knew what he had been up to since then.

Mrs. Fritz told the deputy that, for the past four months, her son had been sharing a condo with two other guys in Algonquin. Although Mrs. Fritz wasn't sure of their names, she was sure that they were ex-cons, just like her son. She had heard - through the grapevine, as she put it - that he did odd jobs for people, which is how he paid his rent. Although she didn't know what kind of odd jobs he did, Mrs. Fritz figured they were probably against the law. Jerry, she said, had never done an honest day's work in his life.

Mr. Fritz still had a soft spot in his heart for his son, Mrs. Fritz told Edwards. Hoping to help, he had deposited a nice sum of money into a bank account for Jerry when he was released from prison for the second time, in 2016. Mrs. Fritz said that the money was gone in a few months. When her son called and asked his father for more, the father decided it was time to wash his hands of any further contact with him.

Mrs. Fritz concluded the conversation by telling Edwards that she figured Jerry was responsible for quite a few of the break-ins that had taken place in the Crystal Lake area.

Mrs. Fritz gave Deputy Edwards the name of the bank where her husband had set up an account and deposited the money for her son. She had no idea if the account was still active, she had told Edwards.

"Yes! Edwards exclaimed loudly, as she hung up the phone.

"What?" Sheriff Fitzgerald asked as he walked out of his office into the bullpen.

"Jerry Fritz's checking account, at Crystal Lake Bank, is still active. I need to take a look at the activity over the past year or so and see if any large deposits were made."

"You'll need a subpoena for that."

"I know. I'm off to see the judge now."

"Well, you better get a move on. It's Friday and he'll be on the links in an hour."

Deputy Edwards jumped out of her chair and headed for the door. "See ya," she yelled.

"Wait," Fitzgerald called out to her.

Edwards stopped and turned towards him. "What?"

The sheriff took a couple of steps closer to her and grabbed her arm. He glanced over to see if Officer Porter was watching and satisfied that he wouldn't be overheard, he asked, "Do you want to get together tonight?"

"I'm sorry, Shaun, but I can't," Edwards told him, as she pulled her arm out of his grasp. "I've got plans."

"What do you have. . ."

"I better get going if I want to catch that judge," Edwards exclaimed and practically ran out of the police station.

Sixteen

Friday

Deputy Edwards had missed the judge by ten minutes. "He's gone for the day," Collin, the judge's clerk, told her.

"What course does he play on?" Edwards asked the clerk.

"Excuse me?"

"I know he's golfing. Where can I find him? What course?"

The clerk stared at her. "You don't seriously think I'm going to tell you where he's at, do you

"It's Turnberry, isn't it? He'd only be playing at a private club and that's the best one around here." She watched the reaction on the clerk's face and grinned. "I nailed it," she said. "Thanks for your help." She turned to leave the room.

"Stop!" the clerk yelled. "You stop right there. I did not tell you where he is and I advise you to stay away from Turnberry Golf Course."

Deputy Edwards grinned. "What are you afraid of? You didn't tell me where he is. I guessed it."

"Please, Deputy, don't go out there. He'll be so pissed off and we'll both be in trouble. And, I'll guarantee that he won't sign your subpoena today or next week, or ever. You should just wait until Monday morning. I'll make sure you're his first appointment of the day."

Edwards didn't say anything for a moment. "All right. I'll back off. But you'll get me in first thing

Monday morning. Right?"

"Actually, I'll do you one better. Judge Nicholson will be in for a few hours tomorrow morning. Can you be here at nine with your paperwork?

"Absolutely, and thanks, Collin."

Deputy Edwards was sitting in a booth at the back of the bar, sipping a rum and coke, when Officer Bill Porter came through the front door. She waved at him and watched as he walked towards her. He stopped at the bar, said something to the bartender, walked over to her booth, and slid into the seat across from her.

"What are you drinking?" he asked.

"Rum and coke. You?"

"Heineken's. Ah, here it is now." He looked up as the bartender set his beer down in front of him. Thanks, Pete."

"No problem," Pete answered and walked back to the bar.

Porter took a long drink, set his glass down, and glanced over at Edwards. "What's going on, Laura?"

Edwards looked down and studied her drink, not saying anything.

"Laura?"

Edwards looked at Porter and shook her head. "I honestly don't know how to answer that, Bill."

"It involves Shaun, doesn't it?" He studied her face, waiting for an answer.

"I'm afraid it does. And, Tic. But, then, it might just be sixteen-year-old news that should be put to rest and I should keep my mouth shut."

"I have no idea what you're talking about, you know. Are you going to clue me in or not?"

"Sorry. Of course, I am." She took a small sip of her drink, looked up at him, and smiled. "This is hard."

"Before you start and just to clear the air, Laura, if this is about you and Shaun. . ."

"What about me and Shaun?" she interrupted.

"Well, I know that you've been messing around with Shaun. And, it's obvious that something is eating you up, but I'm not sure. . ."

Edwards looked surprised. "What do you mean, messing around?"

"Come on, Laura. It's a small office and I'm not blind."

Edward's cheeks turned red, as she blushed. It was only one time and it will never happen again. It was a big mistake on my part and I'm truly sorry it happened."

"Tuesday night?"

"What about Tuesday night?" she asked, confused by his question.

"You and Shaun. It happened Tuesday night, didn't it?"

"How do you know that?"

"Christ, Laura. You both showed up at work looking like hell and hung over. It didn't take a genius to put two and two together."

Edwards looked away, obviously embarrassed. "Ya, you're right. But, that's not what I need to talk to you about."

"So, what is it, then?" Porter inquired.

"I talked with Frances Tickman this morning. She needed some advice and I'm as confused as she is as to what to do. I need your help, Bill."

Porter locked eyes with Edwards. "Tell me," he said, "and, don't leave anything out."

Twenty minutes later, Porter drained the last few drops from the bottom of his glass and set the glass down on the table.

"Well?" Edwards asked.

"There's no question what you have to do. But you already know that, Laura."

"I don't know if I can, Bill. We're supposed to look out for each other, under any circumstances, aren't we? How can I possibly turn this information over to the feds?"

Porter sat back in his seat and shrugged his shoulders. "You don't have a choice. If we were just talking about some porn, I'd say forget it. But there's a murder case involved here. No. There are two murder cases. Marg Finnegan and Tic. And, we're both pretty damn sure that they are connected."

"Bill, if those pictures get out, a lot of families are going to be hurt. Especially, Frances and her kids."

"It can't be helped."

"So, what are you suggesting we do?" Edwards asked.

"Tomorrow morning you and I are going over to Frances' house to get those pictures and a statement from her. On Monday, we'll set up an appointment with the feds and go from there."

"I hate this," Edwards said, her eyes tearing up.

"I know. And, I'm sorry. Do you want another drink?" Porter asked her.

"No, thanks. Two is enough and I'm driving. Where do you want to meet tomorrow?"

"How about The Eggville Café? We could do breakfast before we go over to see Frances," he suggested.

"Sounds good," Edwards said as she stood up to leave. "See you there at what? Eight?"

"Eight is fine," Porter replied and watched as she started to walk to the door.

Edwards stopped and turned back towards Porter. "Shit!" she muttered and walked back to the booth.

"I have a problem," she told Porter. "I'm supposed to be in McHenry tomorrow at nine to get that subpoena signed."

"The one for Fritz's bank records?"

"Right."

Porter thought for a moment. "Well, I want to go with you to see Frances. Can the subpoena wait until Monday?"

"I think that will work. I'll give Collin a call first thing to let him know I can't make it," Edwards said.

"Collin?"

"The judge's clerk. He's a nice enough guy, but you don't want to get on his bad side."

"So, take him some donuts on Monday."

Edwards laughed. "You haven't met him, have you?"

"No. Why?"

"There isn't an ounce of fat on his entire body. I

143

doubt he's ever eaten a donut in his life."

Deputy Edwards pulled into her driveway, got out of her car, and headed towards the back door of her house.

"Where the hell have you been?" a voice yelled.

Edwards, frightened, backed away from the sound. Suddenly, as the man came closer, she realized that it was Fitzgerald. "What the fuck!" she exclaimed, moving away as he reached for her.

"Where have you been, Laura? Do you have any idea how long I've been waiting here for you?"

"Of course, I don't have any idea. Why are you here? We didn't have any plans for tonight."

"Where were you?" he asked again.

"None of your damn business," Edwards said, getting angry. "Now, I'd appreciate it if you'd get the hell out of here. I'm tired and I don't need this shit."

"Were you with another man, Laura?"

Edwards took a couple of steps back, as Fitzgerald reached for her again. "Shaun, I met a friend for a drink. We visited for a little while and I came home. I wasn't on a date and even if I was, it's none of your fucking business. So, back off, will you?"

"Who was he?"

"What makes you think it was a he? It's only a little after seven. If I was on a date, do you think I'd be home already? What the hell is wrong with you?"

"You're sure I don't have anything to worry about? I don't think I could take it if you were seeing someone else."

Getting more concerned by the second, Edwards

took a few more steps away from Fitzgerald. "I'm not seeing anyone. You don't have anything to worry about, Shaun."

Fitzgerald stared at her, not saying anything.

"I'm going in now, Shaun. I'll see you tomorrow."

"Laura," he said softly.

"Good night," she said.

"Can I come in?" he asked, his voice barely more than a whisper.

"Not tonight," Edwards replied. "See you tomorrow. Okay?" She turned and practically ran towards her back door.

Seventeen

Saturday

"Mrs. Tickman, can you tell. . ."

"Please, Officer Porter, call me Frances," she interrupted.

Porter smiled. "Fine. And, please call me Bill."

"What were you going to say, Bill?" Frances Tickman asked.

"Where and when did you find these pictures? How long have you known about this?"

Deputy Edwards held up her hand. "Whoa. Slow down, Porter. One question at a time, please."

Frances, who was standing by the kitchen sink, turned her cup over and poured the rest of her coffee into the sink. "Time for a fresh pot. This tastes like mud."

"Frances, tell me about these pictures," Porter said, pointing towards a small pile of photographs that lay on the table.

"Do you want more coffee?" Frances asked.

"No, I'm good," Edwards replied.

"I'm good, too," Porter said, starting to get antsy. "Can we get on with this? We need to get your statement and get back to the station. The sheriff is going to wonder where we are."

"The sheriff is out of town this morning," Frances said.

"Really?" Edwards said, surprised. "How do you know that? I didn't know that."

"He's on his way to O'Hare. I asked him to give

146

my daughter, Amanda, and her family a ride to the airport. I could have taken them, I guess. Or, they could have rented a limo. But I thought it might be a good idea if he was out of town for a few hours this morning."

Edwards grinned. "You little fox."

Frances smiled back. "I do what I can." She picked up a piece of paper and handed it to Edwards. "Here's my statement. It's not very long. There isn't that much to say."

"Frances, I planned on taping this," Edwards told her.

"Oh," Frances replied, laying the paper back down on the table. "Well, I've written it all down. I guess I'll just read what I've written and you can record it if that's what you want. I've got a signed copy of my statement for you. In addition, I want you to know that I've made copies of all of the pictures. I'm giving you the originals, which are the ones on the table."

"What about the copies?" Porter inquired.

"I'll keep those for now," Frances replied.

"Don't you think you. . ."

"I'm keeping them," Frances said, interrupting him.

Deputy Edwards reached over and switched on her recorder. "This is Deputy Laura Edwards, of the Cary, Illinois Police Department. I am with Mrs. Frances Tickman, who resides at 4748 Hilltop Drive, Cary, Illinois. Also present is Officer William Porter of the Cary, Illinois Police Department.

Today is Saturday, May 29, 2017. The time is

8:57 a.m. Mrs. Frances Tickman has prepared a statement, which she will read at this time. This statement may possibly have some connection to the murders of Marjorie Finnegan and Sheriff Tickman, which are under investigation at this time. Mrs. Tickman, would you like to begin?"

Frances looked at the recorder that had been placed on the table. "Do I just speak normally?" she asked.

"Yes," Porter answered. "You can begin now."

"One week ago today, my husband, Sheriff Richard Tickman was murdered in our home. Richard was a good man and a good husband and father. He served his community well and was loved by many people.

Richard had his workshop out in the garage and spent many hours there. He often told me to stay away from his workbench and tools, saying he was concerned for my safety. I thought it was a little odd for him to tell me this, as I had no desire to tread in his domain, and he knew it. Yet, he would occasionally remind me to stay out of his work area.

A few years ago, I went out to the garage to tell Richard that lunch was ready. His back was to me, and I could see that he was looking at some pictures. When I called to him, he shoved the pictures under a piece of wood, hiding them from me. I told him that his lunch was on the table, he said he would join me in a few minutes, and I walked back towards the house.

What Richard didn't know is that I went back to the garage and watched him through the window. He

148

took the pictures, put them into an envelope, and hid them in a small toolbox, which he then placed on a shelf over the workbench.

I forgot about them. I had intended to check the envelope out some day, but it slipped my mind and life went on. Until last Saturday when Richard was murdered. I don't know why, but the first thing I thought of when I saw Richards laying on the floor in a pool of blood, was that envelope.

The pictures were still in that same toolbox in the garage. I've tried to figure out if Richard took the pictures or managed to obtain them after Marjorie Finnegan's death. I don't know if he was a voyeur or if she knew he was watching and taking pictures. Or, perhaps, she took the pictures and he found them.

Whatever the case, it is obvious that he was one of her sexual partners. Sheriff Fitzgerald, who was a deputy back in 2001, is also in some of these pictures, as are numerous other men."

Frances glanced up from the paper she was reading and looked away. "That's it," she said, tears running down her cheeks. "That's all."

Edwards had all she could do to keep from crying, too. She knew how hard this had been for Frances, as she had seen the pictures of Tic with Marjorie. She looked at Porter, who was reaching over to turn the recorder off.

"Do you have any other questions, Porter?"

Porter sat back and stared at the ceiling, thinking. "You never saw these pictures until after he was dead?"

Frances shook her head no. "I didn't. It's exactly like I told you."

"It's just that these pictures of Tic would give you a reason to want him dead. I'd sure as hell want him dead if he was my husband," Porter said.

"Officer!" Edwards exclaimed. "What the hell are you doing? Frances isn't a suspect."

"Sorry," Porter replied. "I know she isn't. It's just that. . ."

"It's just that – nothing!" Edwards said loudly.

"Forget it, Laura," Frances said. "I know he didn't mean anything by it. Kind of thinking out loud. Right, Bill?"

"I really am sorry. That came out all wrong."

"No harm done," Frances said, smiling.

"Frances, did you search any other part of the garage after Tic died? Or, just the toolbox?" Edwards inquired.

Frances gave her a curious look. "No. Just the box. Why?"

"I don't know. I was just wondering if there could be something else hiding out there."

Deputy Edwards, Officer Porter, and Frances Tickman spent the next hour in the garage. Porter pulled boxes down from the rafters and Edwards and Frances tore them open and searched the contents. They opened boxes that were stored on the shelves and went through tool boxes and drawers.

Starting to get tired, Edwards stretched out her body and let out a big sigh. "I don't think there's anything else here to find."

"There are only a couple more boxes to go. We might as well check them all before we call it quits," Porter told her.

Frances reached into a box, heard a snap, and yelled, "Ouch! What the hell!"

"What?" Porter asked.

Frances pulled her hand out of the box and held it up for Edwards and Porter to see. "A mousetrap. Will someone take this off of my fingers? Please."

Edwards grinned.

"This hurts like hell. I'm glad to see it amuses you, Laura."

"Sorry." She reached over and removed the trap. "What's in that box, anyway?" she asked Frances.

"More boxes," Frances told her. "Some shoe boxes and old cigar boxes."

"Pull 'em out. Let's see what's inside of them," Porter said.

"You take them out. I'm not putting my hand back in there."

Edwards reached down into the large box and pulled out six smaller boxes. She looked up at Frances. "These don't look familiar to you?" she asked.

"Not at all. I have no idea what's inside of them."

Porter walked over to the two women and picked up one of the boxes. He took the lid off and looked inside. "Fuck," he murmured, then immediately turned red. "Sorry," he said.

"What's in there?' Edwards asked him.

"More pictures."

Two of the six boxes were now on the kitchen

table next to the first group of pictures. One box had pictures and one had two pairs of women's panties. The other four boxes were empty and had been left in the garage.

"What are you going to do with them?" Frances asked.

"We have to turn them in with the other pictures," Porter told her.

"But they don't have anything to do with the Finnegan woman," Frances argued.

"Perhaps, the pictures we just found don't, but we don't know about the panties. Are you sure they aren't yours?" Edwards inquired.

Frances puffed up her chest and looked Edwards in the eyes. "Do I look like I would wear those, Laura?"

Edwards grinned. "Hey, what do I know? You're still a good-looking woman. Those panties could be yours."

"Those wouldn't cover half my ass and you know it."

Porter laughed. "I'd like to see the ass they did cover," he said.

"Really?" Edwards said.

"Sorry. Was that out of line?" he asked

"A little," Edwards replied. "The problem, Frances, is that the panties have to be turned in. We'll need to run a DNA test on them." Edwards looked over at Porter. "Bag them."

"What about the pictures?" Frances asked. "Do you have to take them with you?"

Edwards looked at Porter. "They really don't

have anything to do with Marjorie Finnegan. We don't know who this woman is and it's obvious that they weren't taken in the Finnegan house. Also, I'd say that they were taken quite a few years after the ones with Marg. What do you say, Bill? Should we put them aside for now?"

Officer Porter shrugged. "I guess we could keep them under wraps for now."

"Hopefully, we won't need to give them to the feds," Edwards said.

"I'll put them in a safe place," Frances told them, reaching for them.

"I think I'd rather take them with me," Porter said, as he put the pictures back into the box. "Then we'll have them handy if we need them."

"I could make copies of them," Frances said. "What do you think?"

"I don't think that's necessary," Edwards said. "We'll take good care of them. If we need to hand them over to the feds, we'll make copies, then."

"I'd like a set if you don't mind."

"Really, Francis?" Edwards said. "Why in the world would you want these?"

Frances gave her a vacant look. "I don't. . . . I honestly don't know why I said that."

Eighteen

Monday

"I think I'll go with you," Sheriff Fitzgerald said. He was watching Deputy Edwards, who was sitting at her desk filling out another form to obtain a search warrant from Judge Nicholson. Edwards' heart skipped a beat and she fought to maintain her composure. "Why?"

"We're not that busy right now and we haven't spent much time together since Tuesday. I'd like to spend some time with you, that's all." Fitzgerald gave her a strange look. "What? You don't want to spend some alone time with me?"

"It's not that. It's just that I'm really busy right now and. . ."

"What the hell is going on, Laura? Are you pissed at me or something?" Fitzgerald asked, starting to get angry.

Edwards sat back in her chair and looked up at Fitzgerald. "I'm sorry, Shaun, but I think last Tuesday night was a big mistake. You're my boss and it should never have happened. Plus, when you showed up at my house Friday night, you spooked the hell out of me."

"Really? Well, you sure seemed to enjoy what you now think was a mistake. If I remember correctly – and I'm pretty sure I do – you couldn't get enough."

"I was drunk. You know that. I just don't think we should repeat it, that's all."

Fitzgerald. "That's not your decision to make,"

he said angrily.

Edwards stood up and faced him. "I think it is. Now, I'm going to get that subpoena, if you don't mind." She stared at him, waiting for his response.

Suddenly, Fitzgerald gave a nasty laugh and turned away from her. "Do whatever you want, bitch," he said, walked into his office, and slammed the door shut.

"What the hell is going on?" Deputy Larson asked as he looked over at Edwards. "Are you all right?" he asked, seeing the look on her face.

Edwards gave him a weak smile. "I'm fine. Just a little disagreement with the sheriff. No big deal."

"Did I just hear him call you a bitch?"

"Forget it, Larry. It's nothing." She grabbed the form off of her desk and headed towards the door.

"Where are you going?"

"To McHenry, to see a judge. I'll be back in a little while."

Larson studied her face for a moment. "If you need anything, let me know. Okay?" he said, obviously concerned.

Edwards smiled. "I'm fine, but thanks."

Two hours later, Edwards was back at the police station. She knocked on Sheriff Fitzgerald's office door and waited.

"What?" he shouted.

She opened the door a few inches and looked inside. Fitzgerald was sitting behind his desk, staring at her. "What do you want?" he asked, obviously still angry."

"I have the warrant. Do you want me to serve it?" Edwards asked.

Fitzgerald reached out his hand. "Give it to me," he demanded.

Edwards took a few steps towards him and handed him the paper. She waited.

"Is there something else, Deputy?" he snapped.

"I guess not," she replied, turned, and walked out of his office.

Officer Porter glanced over at her and mouthed, "Are you okay?"

Edwards shook her head no, grabbed the keys to her squad car off of her desk, and started walking to the door. She stopped by Porter. "Meet me at noon in Eggville's parking lot," she whispered"

"Do you have the pictures and stuff?" he asked, softly.

"I'm going to get them now. See ya later," she said.

"Porter," Fitzgerald shouted.

Edwards looked back to see Sheriff Fitzgerald standing in the doorway to his office.

"Yes, Sheriff," Porter said.

"Get in here. I have a job for you."

Officer Porter stood up and glanced over at Edwards, who was still watching him.

"Call me," she mouthed, then turned and left the police station.

"What's going on with you two?" Fitzgerald asked as Officer Porter entered the sheriff's office.

Porter gave him a blank look. "What?"

156

"You and Edwards. What's going on?"

Porter didn't reply.

"Don't act like you don't know what I'm talking about. You two seem awful chummy lately,"

"No more than usual," Porter replied. He glanced over at a chair in front of the sheriff's desk. "Should I sit?"

"No." Fitzgerald handed him the warrant. "Take this over to the bank and get all of Fritz's bank records."

"Are you talking about his bank statements?" Porter asked.

"Of course, that's what I'm talking about."

"We already have them," Porter stated.

Fitzgerald looked confused. "What do you mean – we already have them?"

"We found them when we went through his apartment. We have his statements for the last year or so. Fritz kept them, along with a whole bunch of other papers. Forensics is going through everything. They may even be done by now."

Sheriff Fitzgerald sat down behind his desk and shook his head. "What the fuck, Porter. Why didn't I know about this?"

Porter shrugged. "I have no idea. I put the inventory list on your desk."

Fitzgerald thought for a moment. "When did Fritz get out of prison?" he asked Porter.

"About a year ago. His father opened up an account for him at that time. We have copies of all of the statements."

"Was that his only bank account?" the sheriff

asked.

"I'm not sure," Porter said. "I don't think they found anything indicating he had any more accounts any place."

"Well, take this warrant and get over to the bank. Find out if there are any more accounts there that we need to take a look at."

Officer Porter reached for the subpoena. "I'm on my way."

Edwards glanced over at her ringing cell phone, which was lying on the passenger seat of her squad car. Her first instinct was to ignore it, but curiosity won out. She reached for it and hit answer. "Edwards."

"It's me. I'm not going to be able to make our meet," Porter said.

"What's going on?"

"I'm at the bank with the subpoena. It seems that Fritz had a safe deposit box. I'm waiting for a locksmith to get here to drill it open."

"Doesn't the bank have a key?" Edwards asked.

"It takes two keys. The bank's key and the renter's key. We don't have Fritz's key.

Edwards was quiet. "What are you doing after work?" she asked, after a few seconds.

"Nothing. Why?"

"Would you like to go with me to see the feds? If I can set up an appointment, that is."

"I'm in. Let me know." Porter told her.

"Right. Later. . ."

"Wait," Porter yelled. "Don't hang up yet."

"What?"

"Heads up. Fitzgerald thinks something is going on between us. We have to be careful."

"Did he say something?"

"Ya. We have to cool it."

"Got it. I'll talk to you later." She cut off the call and pulled into a strip mall parking lot. She hesitated for a moment and, then, punched in the number for the FBI office in Rolling Meadows.

"That's it!" Deputy Larson exclaimed loudly. "Sheriff," he called out as he jumped out of his chair and ran over to Fitzgerald's office. He opened the door and grinned at the sheriff. "I remembered."

"What the hell are you yelling about?" Fitzgerald asked. "And, you knock before you open my door. Got it?"

Larson stopped dead in his tracks, his face turning red. "Sorry, Sheriff. You want me to go back out and knock?" Larson asked, grinning.

"No, I don't want you to go back out and knock. And, don't be a smart ass. Just remember that the next time. Now, what's so important?"

"I remembered the connection. You know, between Jerry Fritz and Lyle Sleeter." He looked at the sheriff and grinned.

Sheriff Fitzgerald stared at him, waiting for him to continue. "Well?" he finally asked.

"Fritz visited Sleeter when he was in prison. His name is in the visitor log."

"Are you sure?"

"Absolutely. They know. . . I mean, they knew each other."

159

"Do you have a copy of that log, Deputy?" Fitzgerald asked.

"It should be in with the rest of Sleeter's stuff. We put everything back in storage after we determined that he didn't have anything to do with Sheriff Tickman's murder."

"I want to see it."

"I'll get it for you. Funny, isn't it?"

"What's that?" Fitzgerald asked.

"How you can't remember something and you kinda forget about it, and then – out of the blue – it just pops into your head. Strange."

Sheriff Fitzgerald nodded his head. "I guess."

"So, we have a connection between the two. I think we should have a nice long talk with Sleeter. Find out just how buddy-buddy these two were. Whataya think, Sheriff?"

"I think you're right. And, I'm gonna do that first thing tomorrow morning. But, right now, I've got an appointment I need to get to. Good work, Deputy."

Nineteen

Tuesday

"How long have they been in there?" Deputy Larson asked Sally Thompson, the office clerk.

"A couple of hours," Sally told him. "They got here around ten o'clock and they've been talking ever since."

"Do you know what it's all about?" Larson asked.

"I haven't got a clue. Coffee?"

"No, thanks." Larson looked around the room. "Do we have anyone in the back?"

"Nope. It was a quiet night. No arrests."

"Where's everyone else?"

"Patrolling," Sally replied.

"Hey, I understand that Fritz had a safety deposit box. Did they find anything useful when they opened it yesterday?"

"Some money. Quite a bit, I guess. A couple of keys and some documents, which included his will," Sally told him.

"He had a will?"

"Yup."

"How old was he?" Larson asked.

"Thirty-five or thirty-six. Why?"

"I just wondered. A lot younger than me. Maybe, I should have a will. What do you think?"

"I think everybody should have one. It should be mandatory. They should make it the law," Sally exclaimed.

"Why? Not everyone has stuff to pass on or people to leave stuff to." Larson said.

"Maybe. But it sure would eliminate a lot of arguments between families. I remember when my aunt died. She didn't. . ."

Sally and Larson both turned as they heard Sheriff Fitzgerald's office door open. Three men, dressed in black, walked out. Sheriff Fitzgerald stood in his office doorway, watching as they left the police station.

"Is everything okay, Sheriff?" Larson asked him.

Fitzgerald gave Larson a dirty look. "No, everything is not okay. God damn fucking feds!" he yelled. He turned, started to walk back into his office, changed his mind, and walked into the bullpen. "Do you know what those sons of bitches just did?" he shouted.

Deputy Larson gave Sally a questioning look. Sally shrugged and looked down at her keyboard.

"I'll tell you what they did," Fitzgerald said, raising his voice. "They took my case away. They said that they have proof that I might have mishandled the evidence. What the fuck! If anybody mishandled that case, it was Tic. Not me. Said it was now a federal matter and I had to step aside. This is total bull shit." He turned, walked into his office, and slammed the door."

"Do you have any idea what he is talking about? What case?" Larson asked Sally.

"I have no idea. But, if he keeps slamming the door like that - well, one of these days that glass is going to shatter."

"I've never seen him so angry," Larson declared.

Fitzgerald threw open his door, banging it against the wall. "Sally, get everybody in here. I don't care where they are or what they're doing. I want everyone here in thirty minutes. Got it?"

"The entire force or just the ones on duty?"

"What part of everyone don't you understand?" He turned to go back into his office, then, hesitated. "I'm sorry I yelled at you, Sally. Just round up the crew and get them in here. Okay?"

"No problem, Sheriff. I'm on it," she replied.

"What do you think that's all about?" Larson whispered.

Forty-five minutes later, the entire Cary police force, plus the office support staff, were crowded into a small conference room, waiting for Sheriff Fitzgerald to make an appearance.

Officer Porter looked across the room at Deputy Edwards. He watched as she said something to Larson, who shook his head no and shrugged.

Edwards glanced over at Porter, a worried look on her face.

"What's up?" Porter mouthed.

"Don't know?" she mouthed back, then, turned as the door opened and Sheriff Fitzgerald walked into the room.

Fitzgerald glanced around the room. "Everyone here, Sally?" he asked.

"Yes, sir," she replied.

"Good. I'll need you to take notes. Joanne, you can leave. I need you on the phone. Don't interrupt me unless someone is being murdered."

Joanne Beale, one of the office support staff, pushed her chair away from the table and stood up. "Yes, sir," she replied and left the room.

Sheriff Fitzgerald walked to the end of the table. Slowly, one by one, he looked at each one of his officers. "Deputy Laura Edwards will be acting sheriff until further notice. I am. . ."

The room erupted with noise, as the officers reacted to the sheriff's statement.

"Quiet," Fitzgerald yelled. He waited for the room to settle down. "As I was saying, Deputy Edwards will be filling in for me until further notice." He put up his hand as the officers in the room started talking again. "Please. Let me finish."

Deputy Edwards raised her hand.

"Not now, Deputy," he said. Fitzgerald took a deep breath and continued. "As you all know, it is our job to not only protect the public but also to protect each other. Tic lived by this code, as do I. As should all of you." He closed his eyes and waited. "We are supposed to protect each other," he continued. "We are. . ." His voice broke off, and he turned away.

"What's going on, Sheriff?" a voice called out.

"I've been asked to take a leave of absence," Fitzgerald said. "Someone. . . somebody. . . I don't know who. . ." He hesitated for a moment. "Someone has filed a complaint with the FBI, against me. The mayor has asked me to step aside until this matter is cleared up."

"No way," one of the officers yelled.

Fitzgerald looked over at the man. "Way," he said

back to him. "Let me finish this up. Deputy Edwards will be acting sheriff until further notice. You're going to see a lot of the feds around here for a while. They've taken over the Finnegan case. Those of you that were working here at the time of the Marjorie Finnegan murder will most likely be interviewed. I want you to cooperate with them to the fullest degree." He looked over at Deputy Edwards. "I'm sorry I didn't talk to you about this before now, but I only found out about this a couple of hours ago. I've been busy getting things in order. However, as the second-highest-ranking officer, you are next in line for this assignment."

Edwards, looking totally shocked, didn't say anything.

"At this time, Deputy Edwards will continue the investigation into Sheriff Tickman's murder. I expect every one of you to give her your full cooperation. That's it for now. Edwards, I'll see you in my office in five."

Officer Porter walked across the room to where Edwards was standing.

"He could have given me a heads up about this," Edwards muttered.

"Do you think he has any idea who talked to the feds?" he asked her.

"I don't know, but I don't think so," she said. "Shit, Bill. I didn't expect this. I didn't think the feds would come in here like a bunch of stormtroopers and get him suspended."

"Let's just pray that they keep their mouths shut and no one finds out it was us," Porter said. "You better go. He's waiting for you in his office."

"I'm not looking forward to this. What if he knows that I'm the one who turned him in?"

"You'll be fine. Just stay cool."

Twenty

Tuesday

"You again," Mrs. Sleeter declared impatiently, as she opened the door. "Now what?"

Acting Sheriff Edwards smiled politely. "We are so sorry to bother you again, but something has come up and we need to ask Lyle a couple of questions. Is he at home?"

Mrs. Sleeter sighed. "Come on in, but make it fast. We're just about to sit down to eat." She yelled, "Lyle, the cops are here to see you," and went back into her kitchen.

Officer Porter looked at Edwards. "After you, boss."

"That's not even a little bit funny," Edwards told him.

Lyle Sleeter walked into the living room and looked at the two officers. "Sit," he said. "You have more questions?" he asked, as he sat down on the edge of a chair across from them.

"Just a couple. It's about Sheriff Tickman's murder. To be honest with you, we haven't gotten very far. . ." Officer Porter started.

"I don't know anything about that," Sleeter interrupted.

"Of course not. We're not saying you do. We know that Jerry Fritz killed him, and – well, we were wondering what your connection to Fritz is."

Sleeter gave them a blank look. "My what?" he finally asked.

"Your connection to Fritz. Were you friends or did you ever work together or. . ." Porter stopped talking and grinned. "Sorry. I forgot you were only sixteen when you were arrested. So, unless Fritz delivered papers with you, I guess you didn't work together."

Sleeter stared at him. "What the hell are you talking about?" he asked after a few moments.

"Lyle, we have information that Fritz visited you in prison. We're trying to find the connection, that's all."

"You have information? What information? I don't know Jerry Fritz," Sleeter said.

"Then, why did he visit you in prison?"

Sleeter sat back in his chair, as realization suddenly set in. "Oh. You think we were best buds or something and that he visited me when I was in prison. And, then what? You think that we planned Sheriff Tickman's murder and now you think it was me who had that Fritz guy kill him?"

"That's not what we're saying. He did visit you in prison, though. It's in the prison log that he visited you."

"No. He came to visit his brother. I was in prison at the same time as his brother." He stood up and walked to the kitchen door. "Mama, will you come here for a minute?"

Mrs. Sleeter stuck her head out of the door and looked into the living room. "What? I'm putting dinner on the table."

"Mom, do you remember Jerry Fritz visiting me in prison?"

She gave him a confused look. "Jerry Fritz? Why would I. . ." Suddenly, she smiled. "Of course. Well, he wasn't really visiting you."

"Will you please tell these cops why he was there?"

"He was going to visit his brother, Robert. I had a stack of crossword puzzle books I wanted to give to Lyle. I wanted Jerry to ask the guards if it would be all right to give the books to Lyle," she told the officers.

Edwards frowned. "But, how did you know that Jerry Fritz was going to visit his brother?"

"I know his mother. We work the food pantry twice a month. We've been doing it for years. I've never met either one of her sons, but she talks about them all the time. I knew Robert was in the same prison as Lyle, so I gave the books to his mom to give to Jerry. She said she'd have him take them with him the next time he visited his brother and try to get the books to Lyle. Simple enough, isn't it?" She looked at Edwards and Porter. "Is there anything else?"

Edwards shook her head no. "I guess that settles that, then. Thanks for your time, Lyle. We're sorry to have bothered you. Enjoy your meal. It smells delicious."

"I think they are lying through their teeth," Officer Porter declared, as he got into the squad car.

"Maybe. It does sound fishy. Jerry Fritz had to be on Sleeter's visitor list or he never would have been able to see him. They had to know each other."

"I think I should check this out with the warden and see if he can spread some light on this," Porter

169

said.

"Jerry Fritz would have been about nineteen or twenty in 2001. I can't see him hanging around with Lyle back then but, there has to be some kind of connection."

"Looks like we've got some digging to do," Porter declared.

Edwards yawned. "I'm pooped."

"You've had an interesting day, to say the least. How do you feel about this acting sheriff thing?"

"I don't know. It hasn't sunk in yet. Right now, I just want to get home, take a nice hot bath, and go to bed."

"It's only a little after six," Porter said. "Kind of early for bed, isn't it?"

"Hold on," Edwards said and reached for her phone. She looked at the caller's I.D. "Shit! It's Fitzgerald. I'm not answering it."

"Maybe, you should. It's gonna look suspicious if you don't answer his calls." Porter told her.

"I guess," Edwards said and hit the answer key. "Edwards."

"Laura?"

"Yes, Shaun. What's up?"

"What's up? My world is falling apart and you ask 'what's up'?"

"Sorry. How are you doing?"

"I need to talk to you, Laura. Is it all right if I stop over tonight for a little while?"

Edwards didn't answer him.

"Laura, are you still there?"

"Ya, I'm here. I'm sorry, Shaun, but tonight isn't

good. I'm still working and I'm planning on going home and getting a good night's sleep. Some other time, maybe." She glanced over a Porter and mouthed, "What do you think I should do?"

Porter shook his head, "Don't see him."

"Laura, I need to talk to you. Please."

"I'm sorry, Shaun. Not tonight."

"Are you alone?" Fitzgerald asked her angrily.

"Porter is with me. We're just on our way back to the station," she told him.

"Where were you?" Fitzgerald asked.

"At Lyle Sleeter's house."

"What did he say? Tell me," Fitzgerald demanded.

"Sorry, Shaun. You know I can't discuss this with you while you're suspended. I've got to go. Bye." She ended the call and looked over at Porter. "He sounded really upset."

"Don't hang up," Fitzgerald yelled into his phone. "Laura, are you still there?" Angry, realizing that she had hung up on him, he threw his phone across the room. "Bitch!" he muttered to himself.

Twenty-one

Wednesday

"Laura, open up!" Officer Porter yelled as he pounded on the front door of her house. "Laura, are you in there?" he shouted. He glanced back at Deputy Larson, who was standing behind him. "She's not answering."

"Let's try the back door. She's got to be here. Her car is in the driveway," Larson said.

The two men walked to the back door and looked inside the kitchen window. "I can't see anything," Larson commented.

"I'm going to call her phone again," Porter told him, as he pulled out his cell phone.

"Shhh," Larson said. He put his ear to the glass and listened. "I can hear her phone ringing inside the house. She must be in there."

"I'm going in," Porter declared, as he brought his foot back and slammed it into the door.

"That was easy," Larson said, as the door flew open.

"Quiet," Porter said. "Let's find that phone."

They stepped into the living room and listened.

"Her bedroom," Porter declared. "It's coming from her bedroom." They walked down a short hallway to Edwards' bedroom.

"Shit!" Officer Porter said as he saw Edwards' naked body lying on the bedroom floor. He knelt beside her body and checked for a pulse. "She's alive," he yelled to Larson. "Call for an ambulance." As he turned

Edwards over and checked her breathing, he heard Larson talking on the phone. "Tell them to hurry,' he yelled at him.

"They're on their way," Larson said. He knelt beside Porter on the floor and looked at Edwards. "Look at those marks on her neck," he said. "It looks like she's been strangled."

"Bag her hands," Porter said. "And, don't touch anything."

"I know, Bill," Deputy Larson said. "I've done this before, you know."

"Sorry," Porter replied. "I'll call this in. We need forensics out here right away."

Larson looked at Edwards and then glanced over at Porter. "She doesn't look good, does she? What do you think?"

"I think I'm gonna kill the son of a bitch that did this to her," he said.

"What the hell are you doing here?" Officer Porter shouted as he saw Sheriff Fitzgerald walking towards him.

"I just heard about Laura," he replied, as he got closer to Porter. "This is terrible. Who could have done this to her?"

Porter took three steps towards him, pulled back his arm, and swung, hitting Fitzgerald in the jaw. Fitzgerald staggered backwards and went down hard.

"What the fuck are you doing, Bill?" Deputy Larson yelled as he stepped in front of Porter.

"It was him," Porter yelled, trying to shove Larson out of his way.

Fitzgerald, looking dazed, started to stand up.

"Stay down, Sheriff," Larson yelled. He grabbed Porter's arm and pulled him away from Fitzgerald. "What the hell is wrong with you, Bill?"

"Let go of me," Porter demanded, trying to get loose of Larson's hold on his arm.

"Bill!" Larson yelled. "Settle down, will you? What the hell is wrong with you?" he asked again.

Officer Porter pulled his arm loose and walked a few steps away from Larson. He pointed at Fitzgerald. "It's him. He tried to kill Laura."

Fitzgerald glared at him. "You're fucking crazy." He rubbed his jaw and looked up at Porter. "You just hit a superior officer. I'll have your badge for this, Porter," he said, threatening.

"Ya? Well, we'll see what Laura has to say when she wakes up," Porter replied.

Fitzgerald looked like he had been punched in the stomach. "Wakes up? What do you mean, wakes up? I thought she was dead." He stood up and brushed off his uniform. "Larry, do you want to tell me what is happening here? I got a call saying that Laura had been strangled."

"She's in bad shape, Shaun, but she's alive. We're not sure if she's going to make it, but we're all praying pretty darn hard right now."

"You should have been sure you finished the job before you left her house, you prick," Porter told him. "I know you tried to kill her, just like you killed Marjorie Finnegan sixteen years ago."

Fitzgerald gave him a blank stare, then, turned and walked down the hospital hallway toward the exit sign.

"The feds know you killed her," Porter shouted after him. "Your ass is fucked, Fitzgerald."

"It's your ass that's in trouble, Porter," Deputy Larson said.

"That may be. But I know I'm right about this, Larson. It was him. I know it."

"Let's see where the evidence takes us before we jump to any conclusions," Larson said, softly.

"You know you're the acting sheriff right now, don't you?" Porter declared.

Deputy Larson thought about that for a moment. "Ah, shit. You're right."

"Deputy?"

Larson turned and looked behind him. "Doctor?" The look on the doctor's face said it all.

"Nooo," Porter cried out. "Please, god, no."

"I'm sorry. She's gone."

Larson fought to hold back the tears. "Did she say anything?"

"No. She never woke up. I know you don't want to hear this, but it's probably a good thing. If she had come. . ."

"A good thing?" Porter yelled. "How can her dying be a good thing?"

"She would have had permanent brain damage, due to the lack of oxygen to her brain that she sustained when she was being strangled. In other words, Officer, if she had lived, she would have been in a vegetative state for the rest of her life. I'm sorry, but it is a blessing."

Deputy Larson watched as Porter turned and

put his hands against the wall, his body shaking. He looked at the doctor. "Can you give us a few minutes, doctor?" he asked.

"Of course," the doctor replied. "I'll be just down the hall when you're done here.

"Thanks," Larson said. He waited until the doctor was out of hearing range, then, put his hand on Porter's shoulder. "How sure are you that Fitzgerald did this?"

Porter turned and looked him in the eyes. "Pretty damn sure, Larry. Why?"

Deputy Larson stared at him. "You filed the complaint against him, didn't you? You and Laura," he said after a moment.

Porter shook his head yes. "We found pictures of him and the Finnegan woman. Compromising pictures. But, then, we also found pictures of Tic with her. They might have been in it together. We figured the feds were better equipped to take over the case, so we gave them the pictures and the panties to check for DNA."

"Panties? What panties?"

"The ones we found in Tic's garage. Frances found some pictures after Tic was murdered. Laura and I helped her search the garage and we found a bunch more pictures and a couple pairs of woman's panties. Which weren't Frances', by the way." He sighed and shook his head. "It's a long story, Larry. Can we do this later?"

"We are going to do this later," Larson told him. "But, right now, we're going to let everyone know that Laura is awake and talking."

Porter's head jerked up and he stared at Larson. "We're going to do what?"

"I'm going to bring Fitzgerald in and talk to him. I'm going to tell him that Laura woke up and said that it was him that tried to kill her."

"But you can't do that?" He hesitated for a moment. "Can you?"

"I'm doing it. Let's talk to the doctor. I have to be sure that he agrees to keep the news of her death quiet for at least the next twelve to twenty-four hours."

Porter grinned. "I'll be damned, Larry. I didn't know you had it in you."

"Don't get excited yet, Porter. I'm not sure I do."

Twenty-two

Wednesday

"There's no way she said that," Fitzgerald yelled. He looked around the room, totally uncomfortable at being on the other side of the table. He was usually the one sitting where Deputy Larson and Officer Sam Frankel were seated and he was usually the one who asked the questions.

"I'm sorry, Shaun, but she did. On top of that, we found your fingerprints on the front door and inside the house."

"Of course, you did. That's no big surprise. I've been inside Laura's house several times. It stands to reason that my prints would be there."

"Well, we know you did it. The only suggestion I have for you right now is that you tell us your side of the story. It's only a matter of time before the feds find out about this and try to take over. We already know that it was either you or Tic that killed Marjorie Finnegan."

"What the hell are you talking about?" Fitzgerald yelled. "I didn't kill anyone and you fucking know it. And, if you think that one of us killed Marg, you are so wrong."

"Are we? We'll know more when the DNA results are in, but right now you're the one that's alive and you're the one that they're looking at." Larson took a sip of his coffee and made a face. "This shit is cold. Sam, would you mind asking Sally to bring us some fresh coffee?" He looked at Fitzgerald. "How about you,

Shaun? Do you want a refill?"

Fitzgerald shook his head no.

"I'll be right back," Frankel said and left the room.

The minute the door closed, Fitzgerald leaned forward and whispered, "This is bullshit, Larry, and you know it. I didn't kill anyone."

Deputy Larson, looking concerned, shrugged. "I don't know what to tell you. She named you. We have no choice but to arrest you. I think it would be easier on you if you fessed up now and admit you tried to kill Laura. The feds are building a case against you for killing Marjorie Finnegan right now, as we speak. It's gonna go better for you if you cooperated."

"What evidence do they have that I killed Marg? It's been sixteen years and you're telling me that new evidence has shown up. I doubt that very much."

"You know I can't tell you what they found, Shaun." Larson looked towards the door, as Frankel walked in with a couple of containers of fresh coffee. He handed one to Larson. "Careful, it's hot," he said.

"Thanks."

"Sally said to tell you that the feds are on their way in. Somehow, they found out about Laura. She said they were going to stop at the hospital first and talk to her. They'll be here after that," Frankel told Larson.

Larson glanced over at Fitzgerald. "This is your last chance to make a deal, Shaun. Once the feds get here, it's out of my hands."

Fitzgerald lock eyes with Larson, then looked down at the table. "All right," he said, softly.

"Wait a sec," Larson said and reached over and turned on the voice recorded. "Go ahead, Shaun."

"I didn't mean to hurt her. It was an accident." He looked up at Larson. "Really, Larry, it was."

"Go on. Tell me what happened," Larson said.

"I wanted to see her – you know; to just talk. She didn't want to let me in. She said she was tired and she didn't want to see me. What the hell? A few days ago, she was all over me and now, suddenly, she doesn't want to see me?" He coughed and looked at Frankel. "My throat is really dry. Could you get me some water?"

"In a minute. Then, what happened?" Larson asked him.

"I'm dying of thirst here," Fitzgerald said.

"Sam, will you go get Shaun a bottle of water?" Larson asked.

Frankel got up and left the room.

"The recorder's still running. Go on."

Fitzgerald sighed. "I guess I got a little pissed by her attitude and pushed my way into her house. She yelled at me to get the hell out. She was really angry. All I did was try to calm her down. It just got out of hand, that's all. She hit me and I lost it. I guess I hit her back – or shoved her. I'm not sure. The next thing I knew, we were wrestling around on the floor. She was out of control." Fitzgerald put his face in his hands and took a deep breath. "I don't know what happened next. I just lost it. All of a sudden, I was on top of her and my hands were around her neck." Fitzgerald started sobbing.

Frankel walked into the room, hesitated a

180

second, and gave Larson a questioning look.

Larson shook his head no, indicating he should stay quiet. "Here's your water, Shaun," Larson uttered.

Fitzgerald took his hands away from his face and reached for the bottle. "Sorry. I'm so sorry. I didn't mean to hurt her."

"So, what you're saying is that it was an accident," Larson declared.

"Right. You understand, don't you?"

Larson waited while Fitzgerald took another sip of water and put the bottle down. "One thing, though, Shaun," he said.

"What's that?"

"If you were arguing in the living room, how did Laura wind up in her bedroom, naked?"

"Oh, that," Fitzgerald said, chuckling. "Her robe came off during the struggle."

"That's all she was wearing? Just a robe?" Larson asked.

"Ya. She had just gotten out of the tub."

"Wow! That had to be embarrassing?"

"Nah. I'd seen her naked before," he replied, grinning. "She has a great body, by the way," he added.

Deputy Larson stared at him, not commenting.

Fitzgerald looked away. "Anyway," he continued, "she got away from me and ran into her bedroom. Actually, now that I think about it, I think she might have been going for her gun." He paused. "So, I guess it was self-defense – my choking her, I mean. I was just defending myself." He sat back and smiled. "I'm glad she's okay, though. I felt horrible when I heard she was dead." He looked at Larson. "Even though it was self-defense," he added.

"Was it also self-defense when you killed Marjorie Finnegan?"

Fitzgerald jumped out of his chair, picked up the bottle of water, and threw it. "I didn't kill Marjorie," he screamed. "It wasn't me."

"It was either you or Tic and - like I said before - right now the feds are leaning towards you," Larson said.

"It was Tic, not me," Fitzgerald shouted.

"Why would Tic kill her? What's the reason, Shaun?"

Fitzgerald gave him a dirty look. "He never said," he told Larson.

"But you knew about it. He must have given you a reason," Larson told him.

"Okay, so I knew about it and kept quiet."

"That kind of makes you an accomplice, doesn't it? You put an innocent boy behind bars for sixteen years, for Christ's sake."

"I didn't want to get Tic in trouble. Besides, the whore had it coming, fucking around with all those men. Who wouldn't be jealous? I sure as hell. . ." He stopped, suddenly aware of what he had said. "I didn't mean that." He looked at the recorder lying on the table. "Erase that part. I don't know why I said that." He started to reach for the recorder.

"Stop," Larson said sharply. "And, sit back down."

Fitzgerald gave him a dirty look. "I'm still your boss, you know."

"Not right now, you aren't. So, you either sit down or I'll have Sam cuff you to the table."

"This is all bullshit, you know," Fitzgerald muttered, as he sat down.

"That's one hell of a temper you've got, Shaun. It sure doesn't take a lot to set you off, does it?" Larson commented.

"I'm sorry about that. Please, Larry," Fitzgerald pleaded. "Erase that part. I didn't mean to say that."

"Sorry, Shaun. You know I can't do that. So, what were you going to say? Finish the sentence. You sure as hell - what? Were jealous? Is that what you were going to say?"

Fitzgerald looked away. "I've got nothing else to say to you, Larry. In fact, I think I want to talk to an attorney."

"I think that's a good idea. However. . ." He hesitated for just a second. "Officer Frankel, will you please read ex-Sheriff Fitzgerald his rights?"

Fitzgerald's head jerked up and he stared at Officer Larson. "You're arresting me?"

"I am."

"But I just told you that it was an accident. It was self-defense." Fitzgerald whined.

"No, Shaun. It wasn't." He stood up and looked Fitzgerald in the eyes. "It was murder. Laura's dead."

Twenty-three

Wednesday

"The first set of pictures have both Fitzgerald's and Tickman's prints on them. The pictures you found in the garage only have Tickman's."

"Do you know who the second woman is?" Acting Sheriff Larson asked Special Agent Cassidy.

The FBI agent shook his head yes. "We do. It's a Marilyn Weber."

"Who is Marilyn Weber?" Officer Porter asked. "I don't recall anyone from Cary with that name. Unless she's one of the Webers that used to own the hardware store."

"Nope. No connection. She was a hair stylist in some salon in Crystal Lake. She left town about seven years ago. We're still trying to track her down."

"Do you have any idea what her connection to Tic was?" Larson asked.

"We asked around. Her old roommate still lives in the same apartment she shared with Weber. She said that Tickman arrested Weber for public drunkenness. Let her off, though. It never went to court. Looks like she liked to play around and your dead sheriff liked to watch. They made some kind of arrangement. The roommate said it lasted for about six months or so. One day she came home from work and Weber was gone," Cassidy told him.

"How long will it take to get something on the panties?" Porter inquired.

"The lab is rushing it. We should know

184

something in a day or so. You know, don't you, that even if we find DNA on them, that isn't proof of who killed Finnegan."

"I know," Porter said. "Unless Fitzgerald experiences a moment of guilt and confesses, I don't think we'll ever know who did it. Even so, I'd bet my last dollar that it was him. I know what you're gonna say. That they were both screwing her, so it could have been either one of them. But Marjorie Finnegan and Laura were both killed in exactly the same way. That, in itself, is enough to convince me that it was Fitzgerald that murdered both of the women."

"Supposition," the FBI agent declared. "So far, we can't prove a thing."

"Well, it's your case now. We're still working on Tickman's murder and we have diddly squat."

"Let us know if you need some help," Cassidy said, grinning, as he stood up.

"Are you leaving?" Porter asked.

"We are. Thanks for your hospitality." He glanced over at his partner. "Special Agent Fremlock, would you care to escort our prisoner to the car?"

"Can I help you clean out the office?" Sally Thompson asked Larson. "I can box up Tic's stuff and make sure Frances gets it. After all, this is your office now."

"Actually, Sally, I may not be in here that long. The county commissioners need to choose the interim sheriff to fill the vacancy until the next election."

"Well, that may be, but I'm sure they're going to ask you to stay on as acting sheriff. You're the most qualified."

"I guess. I don't know how comfortable I am doing this, though. It's a lot of responsibility. I think Bill Porter would have been a better choice," Larson told her.

"I wouldn't say that. After all, you are the head officer now and you've been around here longer than Officer Porter." Sally looked around the office. "Where would you like me to start?"

Larson shrugged. "I have no idea." He sat down behind the desk and glanced around the room. "Let's not do this today, Sally. I'm not up to it. Let's leave this job for another day."

"Tic has a lot of personal stuff here, doesn't he?" Sally commented. "I wonder if Frances even wants any of it."

Larson reached for the phone on his desk and looked up at Sally. "It's been a rough couple of weeks. I'm going to be here for a couple more hours. Joanne's got the phones. It's almost quitting time. Why don't you go on home and spend an extra hour with your family?"

Sally looked surprised. "Are you sure?"

"Absolutely." He dialed a number and waited.

"Who are you calling?" Sally asked him.

"Frances Tickman. I'm going to ask her if she'd like to stop by one day and pick out the stuff she'd like to keep." He waved his hand at her. "Now get out of here," he said smiling.

"Bye," Sally said, as she closed the door.

"Fran? This is Larry. I have something to discuss with you when you have a minute. Please call me back at the station." He hung up the phone, sat back, stared out the window, and wondered if there was any way in hell he was ready to take on this job.

Larson jumped, as the ringing phone woke him. He glanced out the window, noticed it was already dark outside, and reached for the phone. "Deputy Larson," he answered.

"Frances Tickman is on the phone for you," Joanne Beale told him. "Do you want to take it?"

"Ya. Thanks." He pushed a button on the phone. "Fran. How are you doing?"

"Hi, Larry. I'm fine. I just got home and heard your message. What's up?" she asked.

"A couple of things. First, did you hear about Laura?"

"I did and I think it's horrible what happened to her. I understand that the FBI has taken Shaun into custody."

"They have."

"Good. I hope they hang the bastard."

"They are looking at him for Marjorie Finnegan's murder, also. I think he's probably the one, but it's going to be hard to prove it. He's saying that Tic did it.

"What!" Frances shouted.

"He said he knew about it but kept quiet to protect Tic. Oh, and get this. According to Shaun, Tic was holding the pictures over his head. He told Shaun if he said anything about the murder, he'd make the pictures public.

"I figured Shaun knew about the pictures."

"He did. And, his fingerprints were on them,

too," Larson told her.

"Along with Richard's," Frances added.

"Right. Anyway, the feds have him on withholding information, being an accomplice after the fact, and whatever else they want to charge him with. And, of course, Laura's murder. He won't be seeing much daylight for a long, long time."

"You know, Larry, I always thought there was something a little off with him. Oh, well. What's the other thing?"

"Tic. . . Richard left a lot of personal items here in the office. Sally and I were going to box them up and get them to you. However, I thought it might be easier if you came down here and went through the stuff with us. You could decide what you want to keep and what you want to get rid of. That is, of course, you want to get rid of anything."

"What kind of stuff?" Frances asked.

"Pictures and trophies. There's a whole bunch of trophies. Mostly for bowling and some from the softball league he played on. He may have some things in his locker, too. We haven't looked in there yet. Oh, ya. I almost forgot. One of the desk drawers is locked. Do you know where the key is?"

"Probably on his key ring, wherever that is. I'll look around for it." She was quiet for a moment. "The boys might want some of his trophies," she commented. "I don't want them, but I guess before we throw them out, I should ask the kids."

"Okay. Just give me a heads up when you want to do it," Larson inquired.

"I'll do that. It's a good idea and it will save you

the trouble of hauling everything up here."

"Maybe, we could do lunch after," he said

"Or, I could fix something and we could come back here after."

"That would be nice, but. . ."

"What?"

"Maybe, that's not a good idea right now," Larson replied.

"Larry," Frances said, softly. "Does everyone there know about the pictures with Richard in them?"

"I believe so, Fran. But the only ones that have seen them are us and Bill Porter. And, the feds, of course. Laura saw them, but that's beside the point right now."

"I wonder if we could try to keep this as quiet as possible. I haven't told the kids about them yet, and I don't plan to unless it gets out. There's no reason that they have to know that their father was a pervert," she said raising her voice.

"I'm sorry, Fran. I know this is hard on you. It's been hard on all of us who knew Tic. Would you like some company? I could stop by if you want to talk?" He waited for her response. "Franny, are you there?"

"I'm sorry. I'd love to see you but, I'm kinda pooped. I spent the day with Valerie shopping and she's spending the night here. Thanks, anyway."

"Just call me if you need me, okay," Larson told her.

"I will," Frances said. "I'll call you tomorrow and set up a time to come down to the station. Okay?"

"That sounds good. If I'm not here when you call, just let Sally know."

"Will do. Good night, Larry."

"Good night, Fran," Larson said softly and hung up. He sat back, put his feet up on the desk, and stared out of the window into the darkness.

Twenty-four

Thursday

"When did you get back?" Acting Sheriff Larson asked Officer Porter.

Porter looked up at him. "Sorry, what did you say?"

"Just wondering when you got back. I didn't see you come in."

"I've been back for a while now," Porter told him. "Why?"

"No reason. What are you working on?"

"Tic's bank records. It seems he made some substantial withdrawals over the past few years and I'm trying to account for them."

"What do you consider substantial?" Larson asked him.

"Over a thousand dollars. I may be barking up the wrong tree here, Larry, but I remember Fritz's account having deposits that match up with these withdrawals." Porter gave Larson a questioning look. "You don't think. . ."

"What?" Larson asked.

"Is it possible that Tic was paying Fritz off?"

"Why would he be doing that?" Larson inquired. He hesitated a moment. "No way!" he said, loudly, as realization sunk in. "You think Tic was being blackmailed by Jerry Fritz? Why? There's no connection between the two of them."

Porter looked at the papers in front of him. "The dates agree, Larry. Wait a minute." He reached for a folder and opened it. "No fucking way," he muttered.

"What have you got?" Larson asked.

"Shaun's bank statements."

"When did you get those?" Larson asked.

"The feds found them when they searched his house. I made copies. And, you know what?"

"What?"

"It looks like Shaun might have been paying off Fritz, too. See here?" He picked up a statement and held it up for Larson to see.

"What am I looking at?" Larson asked him.

"Look. Here." Porter pointed to an entry on the paper. "He withdrew twelve hundred dollars on April 1, 2016, and. . ." He reached for another piece of paper. "See, here on Fritz's statement." He pointed at the paper. "See, a deposit for that amount went into Fritz's account."

Larson shook his head. "No way, Bill. Are you saying that Jerry Fritz was blackmailing Tic and Shaun?"

"It sure looks like it to me." Porter sat back in his chair and grinned. "Looks like we've got a motive, doesn't it?"

Larson smiled. "So, what do you think was going on? That, maybe, Tic and Fritz had a falling out and Fritz killed Tic? I guess that's a possibility and it does sound like a motive. It looks like we have a motive and the murderer. Case closed." He slapped the top of Porter's desk. "Damn, we're good."

"It might be closed," Porter said. "Only, do you have any idea what Fritz had on him?"

Larson frowned. "Damned if I know, but what

difference does it make now? Fritz is dead. There's nothing left to do. Right? It's time to put this file away and get back to normal again."

"I guess so. It would be nice, though, if we could tie up any loose strings. I'm just not sure I can put all this behind me until I know the reasons. I'd like to dig a little deeper into Fritz's life. Maybe, we missed something."

"You could be right," Larson agreed. "But I don't think that's going to change anything."

"I'd like to talk to Fritz's mother again if it's okay with you."

"When was she interviewed?" Larson asked. "I'd like to review the notes before she's questioned again."

Porter thought about it for a moment. "I don't know who interviewed her. It wasn't me. Let me check the file." Porter grabbed the file and opened it. He flipped through the sheets of paper. "I don't see anything in here but someone must have talked to her."

"Let me ask Sally if she knows," Larson said and walked over to Sally's desk at the front of the room. Porter watched as Sally shook her head no, and shrugged her shoulders.

"She doesn't know where the report is, but she is pretty sure that it was Fitzgerald that talked to the mom," Larson said, as he walked back over to Porter's desk. "I wonder if he did talk to her," he said.

"He must have. I mean, someone had to talk to her, for crying out loud. Jeez, Larry, this whole thing stinks."

"You think?" Larson replied as he grabbed his

hat and keys. "Let's go talk to that mother."

"I'm telling you for the last time, Caroline Fritz shouted. "I'm not talking to any damn cops about my son. Now, get the hell off my porch."

Officer Porter stared at the woman on the other side of the screen door. He waited while Larson tried to reason with her, explaining that they only had a couple of questions.

"No!" Caroline Fritz yelled. "I'm done with you people."

Officer Porter stepped in front of Larson and smiled. "Mrs. Fritz, we can do this the easy way or the hard way."

"Seriously?" she said, grinning. "You watch too much TV, young man."

Porter smiled. "And, right now you are obstructing justice and we are well within our rights to haul your sorry ass down to the station to question you. The choice is yours. You either talk to us here or, believe me, you will be talking to us there." He waited for a response.

"Officer Porter, I think. . ."

"Wait, Sheriff," Porter interrupted Larson. "I think Mrs. Fritz was just about to say something." He looked over at her and smiled. "Isn't that right, Mrs. Fritz?"

"Screw it," she murmured and opened the door. "Come on in, but make it fast."

"Thank you, ma'am," Porter said, as he followed her into her living room. He turned and looked back at Larson. "Coming, Sheriff?" he asked.

An hour later, the two officers were back at the Cary Police Station.

"Are you sure I can't buy you a drink?" Larson asked.

"Thanks, Sheriff, but I've got some paperwork to do and, then, I'm going over to my mama's for some home cooking."

Larson looked at Porter and smiled. "We did good today, Bill. You did good, I should say."

"We is the right word, Larry. We got the connection and that's the important thing. The pieces are falling into place."

"We got lucky, that's all. I never would have guessed that Jerry Fritz and Marilyn Weber were connected," Porter said.

"I find it interesting that Marilyn Weber had copies of the photos that Tic took of her and those men. Doesn't it seem a little strange to you? A woman having dirty pictures."

"Not really. After all, they were of her. Women can be just as turned on by porn as men," Porter said. "At least, I think they can," he added.

"Whatever the case, at least now we know where Fritz got the pictures he used to blackmail Tic and Shaun. It clears up that mystery," Larson said.

"Perhaps. But we still don't know that Fritz was actually blackmailing them," Porter stated. "We're kind of assuming that's what happened without any real proof."

"Well, I think the pieces fit. All you have to do is look at the bank statements. By the way, are you going

195

to clue the feds in about this?"

"Not today," Porter answered. "Besides, that's your job, not mine." He didn't say anything for a few moments. "Have you heard anything about Laura's funeral?"

"Not yet," Larson told him. "It's hard to believe that we've lost two of our own in less than two weeks, isn't it?"

"Do you know how old she was?"

"Forty-six," Larson answered.

"She looked younger," Porter commented.

Larson stared at Porter for a couple of seconds. "You had the hots for her," he said, grinning.

"I liked her, Larry. Nothing ever happened between us. We were just fellow cops. She was a nice person and I miss her."

"Ya, she was and she devoted her whole life to the force. What a rotten way to go out – killed by a fellow cop."

"Talking about age," Porter said, "how old do you think Frances Tickman is? I think she's a lot younger than Tic."

"Frances?" Larson looked away, thinking. "I know Tic was sixty-two. He married late in life – maybe when he was thirty-eight or forty. I guess Frances is maybe fifty or fifty-one." Larson glanced away. "She's still an attractive woman, don't you think?" he commented after a few seconds. "I wonder if she'll ever marry again."

Porter gave Larson a strange look. "It's kind of soon to be thinking about dating the old boss's wife, isn't it?"

Larson laughed. "Sorry, I'm not talking about me. She's an okay lady, but I like mine a little more on the younger side. No, I'm not interested in her. I was just thinking out loud."

Twenty-five

Friday

"I didn't expect you to come over this soon," Sheriff Larson said, as he took Frances Tickman's hand.

"I just want to get this over with," she told him. "I'd throw every damn thing away if it wasn't for the kids."

"You're angry. I get it."

"Sorry. I guess I just can't get over what he did. God, Larry, how can you live with someone for years and never really know them?"

Still holding her hand, Larson pulled her close into him and gave her a hug. "Just remember that I'll always be here for you," he said softly.

Frances backed out of the hug and looked around the room. "Quiet in here today," she commented.

"Most everyone is out on patrol," Larson said. He smiled. "Are you okay?"

"I'm fine. Shall we get this over with?" Frances replied.

"Let's go," Larson said.

"Shit."

"What?"

"I forget to bring the boxes," Frances told him.

"We've got plenty of boxes here. Don't worry about it. By the way, did you find the key?"

"I have all Richard's keys with me, but I don't know if one of them fits his desk drawer."

"Well, we'll find out soon enough, won't we?"

"Sheriff?" Sally called out.

Larson turned and looked back at her. "What is it, Sally?"

"Do you want some help in there?"

"No, but thanks. Frances and I are fine. Aren't we, Frances?"

Frances smiled at him. "We sure are."

The trophies filled two boxes and Tic's books filled another. The fourth box held several pictures of Tic's family and co-workers. Frances and Larson went through the filing cabinets looking for anything else that might have belonged to Tic.

"That just leaves the desk," Frances said. "Hold on a minute." She reached into her purse and pulled out a key ring that held about a dozen keys. She handed it to Larson. "Pick out the ones that belong here, would you?" she asked him.

Larson took the keys and started sorting through them. "This fits the front and back doors," he said and worked the key off of the ring. "This, I think, is his office key," Larson said, holding up a key and showing it to Frances. He walked over to the door and tried the key in the lock. "It fits," he declared and removed that key from the ring, also.

"What about the desk key?" Frances asked. "Is it that little one?"

"We shall see," Larson replied and tried to insert the key into the lock. "Too small," he told Frances.

"What about that one?" Frances inquired, pointing to another small key on the ring.

Larson tried to insert it into the lock. "Nope," he told her.

"Just force the damn thing open," she told him.

"I'll break the drawer," he said.

"I don't care. I want to see what's so important that he had to keep it here, all locked up," she responded.

Larson looked around the office, trying to find something to use to force the drawer open. "Let me go get a screwdriver," he said. "That should do it."

As soon as Larson stepped out of his office, Frances started opening the desk drawers that weren't locked. She rummaged through the contents, not finding anything of interest. She pulled open the middle drawer and saw a stapler, some rubber bands, pens, paper clips, and a box of staples. She was about to close the drawer when she noticed an envelope under the stapler. She pulled it out of the drawer and opened it. A small key was the only thing inside the envelope. She took out the key and inserted it into the lock. It fit. She turned the key and unlocked the drawer.

"You got it?" Larson said as he walked into the office.

Frances jumped. "You scared me," she said, laughing. "It was in an envelope in the middle drawer."

"Guess I don't need this, then," Larson said and placed the screwdriver on top of the desk. "So, what did you find in there?"

"I haven't opened it, yet," she told him. "Here goes." She hesitated and glanced over at Larson. "What are we looking for, anyway?" she asked.

"I haven't the slightest," he replied. "Something that would give us a clue as to who murdered Marjorie Finnegan would be nice."

"Do you honestly think Richard killed that woman?" Frances asked him.

"I really don't know. But we're all convinced that it was either him or Shaun. We don't have a hell of a lot to go on, and the case is sixteen years old."

"If you had to choose one, who would it be?"

Larson shrugged. "If I had to, I'd say it was Shaun. But we'll probably never know for sure. Are you gonna open that drawer or do you want me to do it?"

Frances pulled the drawer open. Looking surprised, she glanced up at Larson. "It's empty," she said.

Larson reached down and put his hand in the drawer. He tapped the bottom of the drawer and smiled.

"What?" Frances asked.

"The bottom is loose. I think there's something under here." He took the screwdriver, inserted it under the thin piece of wood on the bottom of the drawer, and pried it up, revealing a large envelope. "Got it," he said, excitedly, and took the envelope out of the drawer.

"I'm nervous," Frances told him. "I know it's silly, but I'm not sure I want to see what's in there."

Larson opened the envelope and looked inside. "Pictures," he stated. "It's just a bunch of pictures." He reached in, pulled them out, and turned them face up. As he fanned the pictures out to look at them, his face suddenly went white with shock. He looked over at Frances.

"What is it, Larry," she asked, concerned. "My God, your hands are shaking. What is it?"

Larson shook his head no. "You don't want to see these," he told her, his voice barely a whisper.

"The hell I don't." As she reached for the pictures, Larson held them out of her reach. She stared at him and tried to get her anger under control. "Show - me - those - pictures," she demanded.

Larson grabbed the envelope and shoved the photos back inside. "Believe me, Fran, you don't want to see these."

"For crying out loud, Larry. What's so horrible?"

Larson sat down on the desk chair and shook his head. "Give me a minute. I wasn't expecting this." He took a deep breath. "Would you go get me a bottle of water?" he asked Frances.

"Should I get two bottles, Larry? Am I gonna need one, too? Because I intend to look at those pictures when I come back into this room."

"Then, you better bring two."

Twenty-six

Saturday

Acting Sheriff Larson was tired, and sitting across the table from Special Agent Cassidy was the last thing he wanted to be doing this morning. However, he had called him last night and asked for a meet, telling him he had some news for him.

"This is all a little confusing, Sheriff," Cassidy said, a few minutes after Larson had started explaining Fritz's involvement with the blackmail pictures and the motive for Fitzgerald's murder.

"It's involved, I know, and I don't know if it will help you with the Finnegan case. However, we did find out that Fitzgerald and Tickman were being blackmailed by Jerry Fritz. And, we are positive that Jerry Fritz killed Tickman."

"Is that right?" Cassidy said. "I already knew that Fritz killed him. You told me. At least, I think it was you. However, the blackmail part is new. How did you figure that out?"

"From their bank statements. Withdrawals from Tickman's and Fitzgerald's accounts match up with deposits into Fritz's account. The only explanation is blackmail."

"Well, this is good to know, but, you're right. It doesn't have anything to do with my case." He hesitated, thinking a moment. "But, why did he kill Tickman? What reason did you come up for that?" Cassidy inquired.

"We figure they had a falling out. Perhaps,

Tickman wasn't going to pay him anymore. It could be any number of reasons, I guess. That's why I called you. I'd like you to talk to Fitzgerald and find out what he knows about this. Maybe he can shed some light on it?"

"Actually, our case with Fitzgerald is in the D.A.'s hands. We got everything we need, including his confession to killing Marjorie Finnegan."

"What! What the hell, Cassidy? Don't you think you could have told me that when you got here?" Larson asked, raising his voice.

"I was waiting for the right moment," Cassidy said, grinning.

"This isn't funny," Larson told him.

"Sorry. You just kept talking. I was just waiting for a chance to get a word in. Anyway, it looks like Fitzgerald will be spending the rest of his life behind bars," Cassidy said.

"What reason did he give for killing Marg?"

"Jealousy. Plain and simple. He didn't mind her screwing her husband, but when he found out she was screwing every other Tom, Dick, and Harry in town, he lost it."

"That's probably why he went after Laura, too," Larson said. "He had the hots for her and she didn't feel the same way. It's a horrible thing," Larson said.

"What is?" Cassidy asked.

"Being jealous. It can eat you alive. Some people just can't handle it. I guess Fitzgerald is one of them." Larson looked away, thinking. "Wait a minute," he said after a few seconds. "He must have known that Marg was messing around with other men. What about the pictures Tickman had? Fitzgerald must have seen them."

"Nope. Not until later. That was Tickman's thing, not Fitzgerald's."

"Then, what was Fitzgerald paying Fritz for, if it wasn't about the pictures?"

Cassidy smiled. "You're not gonna believe this one," he said. "Tickman knew that Fitzgerald killed Marg Finnegan. He was making him pay half the blackmail to Fritz. Hell, Fritz didn't care where it came from, as long as he got his money."

Larson sat back in his chair, his mouth open, looking shocked. "No way, man. No frickin' way."

Cassidy laughed. "It's true. Plus, there's more."

Larson gave the agent a disgusted look. "You could have called and given me this information before now, Cassidy. When exactly did Fitzgerald spill the beans about Tickman being blackmailed?"

"It was yesterday. Late afternoon. If it had been sooner, I would have called you but I waited so I could see the look on your face when I told you."

"Very funny. And, they say you guys don't have a sense of humor."

Cassidy smiled. "He finally broke down and told us the whole story," he continued. "He killed the Finnegan woman, and Tickman knew it. Tickman railroaded the Sleeter kid so he could close the case. Tickman wanted to protect his deputy, plus, he needed to make sure his affair with that Finnegan woman didn't get out. So, the two of them reached an agreement to keep it quiet. Then, a few years later, Tickman did the same thing with Marilyn Weber."

205

"Taking pictures of her having sex with men," Larson interjected.

"Right. She shows the pictures to Jerry Fritz, who proceeds to contact Tickman and asks for money, telling him he'll show the pictures to the newspaper if he doesn't pay up. Tickman agrees to pay, but it gets out of hand, and he's already dipped into his retirement fund. He tells Fitzgerald that he has to pay half of the blackmail money. They had each other by the balls, so to speak."

"I'm surprised one of them didn't just make Fritz disappear," he said, smiling "I didn't think we'd ever find out which one actually killed Marjorie Finnegan. How'd you get Fitzgerald to talk?"

"We have our ways," Cassidy said, smugly.

"So, I guess, that's it, then. Both cases are closed." Larson commented.

"I guess," Cassidy replied. He started to get out of his chair, then sat back down, and looked at Larson. "Are you absolutely positive that Fritz killed Tickman?"

Larson looked surprised. "Of course, I am. We all believe he did it. His prints were in the house."

"I know that. But, did you know that Fritz was in Tickman's house earlier that day?"

"Earlier what day? What are you talking about?

"The day Tickman was killed. Fitzgerald told us that Fritz and he met Tickman at his house that afternoon. They told Fritz if he wanted to make some money, they had a job for him."

"What kind of a job?" Larson said, looking confused. "What are you. . ."

206

"There was no job. They only told him that to get him to show up," Cassidy continued. "When Fritz got to Tickman's house, they told him that they were done paying him. They'd had enough. Threatened him, I guess. Fitzgerald said Fritz took it okay. Said he understood and he would keep his mouth shut about the pictures. He took their final payoff and left." Cassidy took a sip of water and grinned. "And, that, by the way, is how Fritz knew there was a safe in Tickman's house. According to Fitzgerald, Tickman made some kind of a comment, in front of Fritz, about getting the money out of his safe."

"I'll be dammed. So, that's how he knew it. But, Tickman's son said he walked right to it. How did he know where it was?" Larson asked. "

"I'm not sure. Obviously, he didn't know where it was when he was there robbing the place during the funeral."

"Well, if John Tickman was telling the truth about that, he found out somehow. I guess, Fritz was pissed off about losing his gravy train and he came back later that day and killed him," Larson said.

"That sounds about right. It's as good a reason as any. But, no matter how it went down, Fritz's prints were already in the house before Tickman was killed."

"Right," Larson said. "I guess when he was there that day, he probably decided there were a few things worth stealing and came back to rob the place during the funeral."

Cassidy got up out of his chair and smiled. "It's your case. If you want to accept Fritz as Tickman's killer and close the case, that's up to you."

"You don't think he did it?" Larson asked, obviously getting upset. "Well, then, who do you think did do it?"

"I haven't got a clue," Cassidy said. "I'll be off now," he said, as he reached out to shake Laron's hand. "Nice working with you."

"You, too," Larson replied. "Thanks for your help."

Larson watched Cassidy walk out of the building. He leaned back in his chair, put his feet up on the conference table, and smiled. "That's right, you prick. You don't have a clue. You don't have shit," he said, in barely a whisper. He closed his eyes and started to drift off.

"Sheriff?"

Sally's voice brought him back to reality. He opened his eyes and looked over to where she was standing in the doorway. "What is it?"

"Laura's service is in an hour. I just thought I'd remind you," she said.

"I know," he replied. "I'm just getting my thoughts together. I'll be right there."

Twenty-seven

Saturday

The memorial service for Deputy Laura Edwards was short. A few close friends and family spoke, relating stories of Laura when she was young and how all she ever wanted was to be a cop. Some of the stories brought laughter, but the final song, *Just a Closer Walk With Thee*, brought tears to everyone's eyes. A light luncheon was served in the church basement.

The majority of the Cary Police Department attended her funeral, some still reeling from the sudden deaths of two of their fellow officers and the arrest of Sheriff Fitzgerald. The cops that needed to get back to work paid their respect to Laura's family and left. A few of the off-duty officers stayed for the luncheon.

Acting Sheriff Larson was seated at a table with Frances Tickman and a few of his fellow officers, enjoying a cup of coffee. They were discussing the fact that a cop never knew, when he walked out of his house that morning, if he'd make it back home that night.

"That's very true," Porter said. "But Tic and Laura were both killed in their own homes. I guess in a sense they died in the line of duty. Or, did they?" He looked at Larson. "What do you think, Larry?"

"I don't know. Tic was a good cop, but he got himself into a real mess. It all went to hell and now he'll be remembered as a dirty cop." He looked at

Frances. "I'm sorry, Frances, but it's true."

She looked away. "I know," she said.

"I'm still finding it hard to digest that he covered up the Finnegan murder." Larson continued. "And, I get sick every time I think about Fitzgerald killing Laura. The only thing I get out of all of this senseless shit is that you never really know someone."

"I guess," Porter said. He looked across the room at the table where Laura's parents were sitting. "I feel so sorry for the Edwards family. Especially, her parents. Parents aren't supposed to bury their children." He bit his lower lip, trying to hold back his tears. "Sorry," he said, as he got up from the table. "I need a minute."

Larson watched as Porter walked away from the table. "He really liked her," he told Frances. "I think they might have gotten together down the road."

"We all liked Laura," Frances commented. "She was a nice person and a good cop. Richard always spoke highly of her."

"Sorry," Larson said, as he reached for his cell phone. "I need to take this." He stood up, answered his phone, and walked away, passing Porter who was returning to the table. "What?" he shouted, drawing attention to himself. He mouthed sorry and walked out of the room.

"How are the kids doing?" Porter asked Frances.

"They're doing okay. Still trying to adjust to the fact that their dad is gone."

"We all are," Porter looked up as the other two cops at his table stood. "You guys leaving?" he asked.

"My kid has a baseball game," Officer Frankel

said. "See ya."

"You, too," Porter replied. "What are you up to for the rest of the day?" he asked the other cop, Steve Santinni.

"Gonna go watch his kid play ball," he told Larson, smiling. "Take care, Larson."

"Thanks for coming, guys."

"We need to leave, Bill," Larson, said as he approached the table. "Something's come up. Sorry, Frances, I won't be able to drive you home. Can you find a ride?"

"No problem," she answered. "What's up?"

"That was Sally. Marilyn Weber just called the station. She says Jerry Fritz was with her when Tic was murdered.

Officer Porter looked shocked. "You're kidding."

"God knows, I wish I was. Let's go."

"Jerry couldn't have killed him," Marilyn Weber told Larson. "I was in town that week. Well, not the whole week, but I was with Jerry from Wednesday to Saturday night. I left early Sunday morning. I didn't hear about his death until a couple of days ago."

"Who did you hear it from? Sheriff Tickman's death, I mean."

"My old roommate. She told me," Marilyn said.

"Marilyn, we looked for you and we couldn't find any record of where you've been working or where you are living. Where have you been these past few years?" Porter asked.

Marilyn looked at Porter and, then, glanced over at Larson. "I seriously don't know how much to tell you. I mean, I knew Sheriff Tickman. That's why I was so surprised to find out he was dead. But I mean – like, I don't want to say anything bad about him." She looked at Larson. "I don't know what you want me to say, Sheriff."

Larson glanced over at Porter. "What do you think?" he asked.

"I think we should tell her what we know," Porter replied.

"Tell me what?" Marilyn asked.

"This may help," Larson said. "We know that you and Tickman had an affair and that it lasted about six months. We know about the pictures and that your boyfriend, Fritz, was blackmailing him."

"First of all," she replied, "I didn't have an affair with Sheriff Tickman."

"But you screwed around with him," Larson stated.

"Yes. Through no choice of mine. And, Fritz wasn't my boyfriend," she said.

"Are you saying you didn't have an affair with him either?" Larson inquired.

"No." She sighed and sat back in her chair. "Yes. I don't know. He was more like a friend with benefits. You know what I mean. So, no. It wasn't an affair. I had a lot of boyfriends back then. Jerry was just one of them. But, after I got busted by Sheriff Tickman and we made that deal, it got out of hand. He was sending his friends my way. I got tired of it and, to tell the truth, he scared me. So, one day, I packed up my stuff and left town."

"He was pimping you out?" Porter asked her, a

surprised look on his face. "How many. . ."

"That's enough, Officer," Larson said.

"Sorry. Where were you, anyway?" Porter asked.

"I have an aunt and uncle who live west of here," she said. "I've been staying with them. It's been great." She laughed. "I've learned how to milk a cow and ride a horse. I breathe in fresh air and mostly go to bed when the sun goes down. I'm not the person I used to be, Sheriff Larson. The best thing I did was to get away from here, and I intend to go back."

"You said you were with Fritz from. . ." Larson thought for a moment. "Wednesday to Saturday. Did you stay with him?"

"Ya, at his apartment."

"And, you said you spent the entire day with him on Saturday. Is that right?"

Marilyn shook her head no. "Not the whole day. He went out for a while in the afternoon. He said he was meeting someone. But we did spend the rest of the day together. Night, too."

"Give me the timeline," Larson asked her.

"For Saturday?"

"Right. For Saturday," he answered.

Marilyn thought for a moment. "We had breakfast at Denny's at about ten or so. We were there for about an hour and a half. We just talked. Then, he dropped me off at a friend's house."

"What time was that?" Larson asked.

"Around twelve or so. She lives in McHenry, so it was a little drive. And, he picked me up around four-thirty or five."

"Then, what?" Porter inquired.

"We spent the rest of the day together. We had dinner at his mom's and I left Sunday morning."

Porter stared at her. "Would you testify, under oath that you were with him between five-thirty and seven o'clock?"

Marilyn Weber looked Porter in the eyes. "I most certainly would."

Larson stood up and started pacing the room. "We talked to Fritz's mother, Marilyn. She never told us any of this. She said she didn't know anything except that you and Jerry were friends. Why do you think that is? Why do you think she didn't tell us that he was with you?"

Marilyn shrugged. "The only thing I can think of is that she hates cops. I mean, she really hates cops. Or, maybe, she didn't know. We ate late. I don't think we ever talked about what Jerry and I did earlier in the day. She probably didn't know, now that I think about it."

"You know what this means, don't you?" Porter said.

"I wish that woman had never shown up," Larson declared. "Do you believe her?"

"I'm torn," Porter replied. "She's believable, yet none of it makes any sense. Just the fact that Fritz's mother didn't speak up and defend her son is suspect. I mean, can a person hate the cops so much that they'd let the world believe her kid killed someone? That's a little far out if you ask me."

"You know I've closed the case," Larson said.

"I know," Porter replied. "What are you going to

do?"

"I'll check out her story, but it's not a priority. If I find any truth in it, I'll have to rethink everything. But, right now, I'm considering the case closed. This station has to get back to normal. We have to start to heal and that's not going to happen if we keep drudging up all this shit."

"That's it, then?" Porter asked.

Larson smiled. "That's it. At least, it is for now"

Twenty-eight

His heart was pounding. Larson rolled over onto his back and took a few deep breaths. "I swear to god, woman, you're gonna kill me."

"It's been almost six weeks, Larry. I've got a lot of catching up to do."

"You mean we, don't you?" He turned on his side and looked into her eyes. "I have missed this." He kissed her on the cheek, still trying to catch his breath. "I have got to start exercising."

"This is when I seriously miss smoking," she said. "There's nothing like a cigarette after a good fuck."

Larson laughed. "It was good, wasn't it?"

"The best." She took his hand and laid it on her breast. "God, I just can't get enough of you."

Larson started to gently tweak her nipple, watching as it got hard.

"That feels nice," she told him. "Harder."

Larson slipped his hand between her legs and gently started to massage her. She moaned and started to move her hips back and forth, keeping in time with his rhythm. "Don't stop," she whispered.

He pulled his hand away and laughed. "You never get enough, do you?" He swung his legs over the side of the bed and stood.

"Fuck you, Larry," she said, joking. "Where are you going?"

"To turn down the damn air conditioner. It's hot in here."

"That's because you throw off so much body

216

heat."

Larson turned and stared at her naked body. He smiled.

"What are you smiling about?"

"I love your body. I could look at you all day."

She grinned. "You're easily pleased. Bring me something to drink, okay?"

"Water?"

"That's fine." She started to pull the sheet up over her body. "Wait. Is there any wine left?"

"A little. Are you staying the night?" he asked.

"Do you want me to?"

"Not really. I have to get up early and, if you stay, I won't get any sleep."

"All right, then. I guess I'll go home. But, I'd still like that wine."

"Nope. You're driving."

"You're not my father, you know," she said, grinning.

"I just want to be sure you're around tomorrow."

"Why? What's tomorrow?" she asked.

"I plan on doing this again. And, then, the day after that and the day after that."

She laughed. "Okay, I get it. Just bring me a glass of water, please."

As soon as Larson left the room, she reached over and pulled open the top drawer of the nightstand. She picked up a stack of photos and started flipping through them. She stopped when she found the one she was looking for and stared at it. Within seconds, she felt herself getting wet. She reached down and touched herself.

"Get your hand out of there," he said, laughing. "Why are you looking at those again?" Larson asked as he handed her a bottle of water.

"They turn me on," she said. "I want you one more time before I leave, and these pictures get my juices flowing, sweetie."

Larson laughed. "Everything gets your juices flowing. But I'm still trying to replenish some of my fluids, so it's gonna be a few minutes."

She held up a picture for Larson to look at. "This is my favorite one," she said. "Look at how our bodies fit together. But it's the way you're looking at me that I love."

Larson smiled. "It is one hell of a picture, isn't it?"

"This picture had to be taken at least a year ago." She sighed. "Can you even imagine what would have happened if someone else had found these pictures in that desk drawer?"

"I don't even want to think about it. We got lucky, that's all. I still can't believe that Tic knew about us and never said anything."

"I guess he liked to watch more than participate. Our sex life ended a long time ago. But, then. . ." She thought for a moment. "My god, it just dawned on me. He lost interest in having sex with me about the same time we started seeing each other. Do you think he knew about us the entire time?"

"If he did, he sure hid it well," Larson said. "He didn't seem any different towards me in the past couple of years than he did when I first met him. I don't know if I could be that cool if I knew someone was screwing my wife."

"I just don't know how he managed to get these shots of us. My god, Larry, he had to be hiding in your closet."

"He had balls. You gotta give him that." Larson took another long swallow of water.

"Maybe. But it creeps me out," she told him. "How much longer do you think we have to wait before we let people know we're dating?" she asked.

Larson smiled. "Is that what we're doing? Kind of a backward relationship, don't you think? First, we screw around and then we date?"

"You know what I mean," she said.

"I'd like to wait until after I get appointed sheriff."

"Are you sure you're gonna get it?"

"That's the word on the street. It makes sense. I'm acting sheriff now, and I'm the next in line. Elections won't be held for another two and a half years. By then, I should be a shoo-in." He grinned. "I do believe it's in the bag."

She took a long swallow of water. "Larry?" she said, dragging out his name.

"Yes,"

"Why did you cut off Richard's penis after you killed him?"

He looked surprised. "You don't know?"

"Well, I think I might, but I'm not sure."

"I did it because he hurt you. It still pisses me off, knowing he cheated on you with those women."

"Oh." She looked away. "But, on the other hand, I cheated on him with you."

"It's not the same," Larson told her.

"It isn't?"

"No. You never would have done it if he had been faithful to you."

She thought for a moment. "I'm not sure about that," she said, smiling.

Larson gave her a surprised look. "What are you saying?"

"You're hot, that's all. I wanted to jump your bones for a long time before we got together."

Larson laughed. "Right, I'm the hot one." He glanced down at her.

"Sometimes, I feel kind of bad about the way he died. He wasn't all bad, you know. I wish you wouldn't have had to kill him."

"You could have divorced him, you know," Larson told her.

"I know, but then I would have had to split everything and now I get it all plus his pension. I wouldn't have gotten that if I'd just divorced him."

"Well, I don't miss him and you shouldn't either. He was a pervert and he got what he deserved. I'll tell you this; he certainly didn't deserve you."

She smiled at him. "I love you, you know."

"I know," he replied.

"It's funny how everything worked out, isn't it? With Fritz going back to the house and all."

"Hell, if John hadn't shot him, everyone would still be trying to figure out who killed Tic. There still are a few people who know it wasn't Fritz who did it," Larson said.

"You mean Porter and that Weber woman? And,

there's Fritz's mom, don't forget."

"I've got it under control. Don't worry. It couldn't have gone any better if we had planned it. As I said, we got lucky." Larson declared.

"What about that Weber woman? Could she be a problem?"

"I think we're good. She's not in the area anymore. I'll keep tabs on her. If she shows up, I'll deal with her then. Right now, I don't want to make any waves."

"I guess," she said, putting her arms up over her head and stretching.

He looked down at her. "Why'd you cover-up? I like looking at your naked body."

"Well, a little modesty never hurts," she said, smiling, as she threw back the covers. "But, just a little."

About the Author

I was born in Idaho in 1939. My father's job demanded that we frequently move. So, by the age of ten, I had lived in Idaho, Montana, Colorado, Michigan, and finally Wisconsin.

I am the proud mother of three wonderful sons and two fantastic grandsons. I have no plans to acquire another husband, as they are just too much work.

For most of my life, I worked as an accountant. Two years before I retired, I did a complete switch in careers and managed two Curves fitness facilities in Illinois. I retired in 2002 and moved to Branson, MO. In 2012, I moved to Indiana to be closer to my family and have resided in Highland since then.

I enjoy a good laugh and figure it's my sense of humor that has kept me going when times were tough. Reading has always been one of my passions and I still read a couple of books a week.

Previously, I just wrote poems for amusement. In 2014, I wrote my first book, *Blueberries and Bears and My Brother's Shoes*, a book about growing up in the forties and fifties. After I self-published it and gave it to friends and family to read, they encouraged me to get serious about my writing.

The Mayor's Son, my eighth book, was a trip back memory lane, as it takes place in my old hometown in Wisconsin. It's a battle of wits between the chief of police and one of his cops.

Crossing Sydney, my first novel was published in July 2015. It has received outstanding reviews.

Don't Smother Your Mother, A Bad Week in Hollister, and *Floating Face Down,* are the Sheriff

"Cowboy" Berkson series. I wavered a lot about the ending the series, as I knew it meant the end of writing about some of my favorite characters. However, I figured there are a lot of other people roaming around in my head that can wind up in a book. So, I sadly said goodbye to Cowboy and the cast of characters in the three-book series.

Let's Play Autopsy, my fourth book, takes place in Kalispell, Montana. The persons and places are fictitious, although at one time when I was quite young, I lived in that city.

Cowtown is my sixth mystery novel. It takes place in a made-up Chicago neighborhood. The Campanales are an unusual family, who mistakenly think they are more qualified to take care of the town bully than the cops. Never a good idea, as they soon find out in this exciting story with an unexpected ending.

Willerton Woods is my seventh mystery novel. My dad hunted in the Upper Peninsula and we made yearly trips before hunting season to spruce up his deer blind.

I never thought that, at the age of 76, I would become an author. I certainly am enjoying my retirement knowing, when I get up each morning, I have something to look forward to.

You can find out more about me and my books at www.susanlpare.com. Please visit me there and feel free to send me your comments.